# I'll Toss You For It!

Rowland McGabhann

## *Also By*
### Rowland McGabhann

Fiction:
*Come 'ere I've got an Idea*
*I've Got it Covered!*

Non-Fiction
*Releasing the Beast Within*

# I'll Toss You For It!

Rowland McGabhann

DoctorZed
Publishing
www.doctorzed.com

This edition Published 2023 by DoctorZed Publishing.
www.doctorzed.com

Books may be ordered through booksellers or online:

ISBN: 978-0-6456529-0-1 (hc)
ISBN: 9978-0-6456529-1-8 (sc)
ISBN: 9978-0-6456529-2-5 (ebk)

Cataloguing-in-Publication entry can be found at the National Library of Australia.

Cover image Australian Flag © Amarosy | Dreamstime.com
Cover design © Scott Zarcinas

rev. date: 18/02/2023

*To the real 'Rambo'. Still getting it done.*
*And to 'Simon' of Coober Pedy for telling it like it was*

# ACKNOWLEDGEMENTS

Thank you to the team at DoctorZed Publishing for all their support in getting this book published, and especially to Dr. Scott Zarcinas for his insight and wisdom in the art of storytelling. Thank you also to everyone who provided 'real time' advice on location and current police practice.

## PROLOGUE

## ADELAIDE, AUSTRALIA
## 1972

They caught the first sight of their new home as they stood on the deck of the HMS *Australis*. The ship that had carried them around the world from their home in Spain.

The ship's captain married Diego Suarez and his wife Monica shortly after boarding back in Southampton weeks ago, which seemed to them so long ago. They clasped hands as they gazed with wonder, watching the sun rise over the distant hills to reveal the vast, strange land where they would begin their new life.

It had all started with a miraculous discovery back on their home on the Island of Mallorca.

Diego was a caver, or as they were nicknamed 'Cavernicola' (Caveman), a slur on their miserable existence, where they eked out a living by bringing amateur explorers to the caves that pockmarked the volcanic island.

The discovery of lost Nazi loot allowed them to escape their drab existence. They were forced to do something due to family disapproval of their relationship.

He had only taken enough to give them a start in the new world, a friend of his had been pressuring them to come with him to Australia. He had told them wonderful stories of people getting rich mining for opals in a place called Adelaide, so when they discovered this, they decided to take him up on his offer.

That world seemed a lifetime away as they stood on the liner's deck as it made its way to the harbour in Port Adelaide.

They could barely contain their excitement, mixed with trepidation, as the tugs maneuvered the ship alongside the quay. Finally, it was time to disembark, it seemed to take forever, but at last, they had made their way down to the quayside, joined by their friend and his wife, Felipe and Rosa Herrero.

They were a bit older but had gotten on well on the trip. He had filled their heads with stories of the wonders of this country provided by this contact, a friend of his had emigrated here a couple of years ago. He was a contact to help them get started. So, they were very much in his hands.

They filed into the customs shed and were directed to an emigration officer. The line moved quickly, and when they arrived at the offices, he barely glanced at them when he stamped their passports.

'Welcome to Australia,' he said, handing them their documents. Before they knew it, they were outside the terminal waiting for their friend to join them.

With their luggage at their feet, they stood surrounded by a bewildering array of different nationalities, all with the same bewildered look.

'Okay, we have to catch the bus to the central station in Adelaide,' Felipe instructed as he took charge.

The line for the bus seemed to go on forever, but eventually, they boarded and, much to their surprise, arrived at the station in about forty minutes. Disembarking, they collected their luggage, then Diego turned to his friend and his wife.

'So, this is it, we have arrived?' he asked in Spanish, as his English was limited.

Felipe laughed, 'Not yet. We have to get another bus. Come on, let's buy the tickets.'

They made their way to the counter. 'Four tickets to here,' he said, indicating a place written on a piece of paper he had.

'You are in luck. There is one leaving in an hour,' the guy at the desk informed them.

'Will we be there before dinner?' Monica asked. She spoke the best English of all of them.

The guy laughed, 'Depends on what day you are talking about!' as he turned to serve the next person.

The four made their way to the bus. Monica asked, 'How far is this place, and what is it called again?'

'It's called Coober Pedy. I am not sure how far it is, but we have to change bus to a place called Port Augusta. We can ask the bus driver.' But as they boarded, they had no chance to ask the driver as they hurried along to their seats. They settled in and began to take in this new world's sights.

The bus was soon passing through the outskirts of the city. The countryside soon morphed into a vision of dry flora, which was indicative of this dry state. 'Has there been a fire?' Rosa asked.

Felipe laughed as he tried to display his knowledge of this land. 'No, this is how the land looks here. I have been told it is the driest state in the second driest continent in the world. Water is precious here. They have to ration it sometimes.'

They lapsed into silence as they realised that place was like another planet to them. After what seemed a lifetime, travelling vast distances through some of the same sunburnt landscape, they had passed through small townships which, from what they could see, had few inhabitants. Finally, they pulled into Port Augusta and disembarked at the bus station.

'I have never travelled so far on a bus. How long was it?' Diego asked his pal.

Felipe looked at his watch and replied, 'Three and a half hours. Can't be much further to our stop.' There was what sounded like a little bit of doubt in his voice. 'I will go and check on the time for our next bus. Do you want to help, Monica? You have the best English.'

She nodded, and they headed over to the office. A surly-looking gent was sitting behind the desk, watching football on the TV.

'Excuse me, could you tell us what time the bus for Coober Pedy is leaving?' Monica asked.

Without looking up, he glanced at his watch, 'About forty minutes,' he replied.

'Oh, one more thing, could you tell me how long the journey is?'

A strange look came across his face as he dragged his attention away from the TV. 'You are not from around these parts, are you?'

'We are from Spain,' she replied, deciding Mallorca would be too hard for him.

'And I suppose you are going to Coober Pedy to make your fortune,' he said, and burst out laughing.

'What's so funny?' she asked. 'I only wanted to know how much further it was. We have been travelling for the last three and a half hours, and we are anxious to get to our destination.'

He stood up, not used to having a sprat of a girl speak back to him. 'Well, you better get yourselves ready for a bit more. It is five and a half hours to that hell hole, so settle in and enjoy the trip,' as he shut the door of the office.

'Five and a half hours,' they gasped.

'What time is it now?' Diego asked.

Felipe replied, 'Nearly midnight. It looks like we have a long night in front of us.'

After what seemed to be a lifetime, the bus finally started to vary its speed. Stretching themselves as they rubbed the sleep out of their eyes, the glanced out the window to be greeted by a landscape that resembled the surface of the moon!

'We can't be here yet. All I can see is a few sheds,' Diego grunted.

But Monica poked him on the shoulder, pointing to a monstrous sign with the words 'Coober Pedy' emblazoned in giant letters.

'But where is the town?' Felipe asked.

One of the passengers leaned over, 'First time, yeah? Well, it's all underground, too hot to live on top. So, seeing as we are digging holes for opals, we might as well dig out a house at the same time.'

While they tried to come to terms with this, the bus stopped in front of one of the few sheds that dotted the landscape. As they stepped out, surveying this strange place, Diego turned to the other three, put his hands on his head, and yelled, 'We have come halfway around the world to escape the caves and we are right back where we started!'

# 1

## MALLORCA, SPAIN
## PRESENT DAY

Charlie was sitting in his local, 'The Blue Bar.' He had arrived there, as he did every morning after going through his daily ritual of a run on the beach, followed by a coffee and croissant.

His brothers, Des and Vincent, had just joined him. They had become known locally as the Savage brothers, not as the name implied, by their actions, but rather because it was their surname. But the confusion could have excused anybody who had been following their escapades.

It was nearly six months since they discovered a plot to recover some lost Nazi treasure, but now Chaz was feeling itchy.

'I am bored out of my mind,' he mused as he stirred his coffee.

'That won't last. Maria tells me that they have located the ship that transported her aunt and Diego to Australia,' Des informed them. 'All they are waiting for now is any information as to where they settled,' he added.

'It could get a lot worse,' Vincent added. 'Ma has got it into her head to try and locate her mother's brother, who, according to the story, related to her many times when her mum would have a few sherries and launch into the tale of how her brother had to immigrate to Van Diemen's land, Adelaide, because he had "took up with Lady white", a protestant woman, something that was frowned upon at that time. So now that the search is on for the Heart's family, she wants to get in on the act.'

'In Adelaide, that can't be a coincidence that they both headed for the same place. Australia is huge. What are the chances of them heading to the same destination?' Chaz commented.

Des decided to fill them in on the history of immigration there, based on all the research the Hearts had done.

'Voluntary immigration began with Adelaide being the chosen destination, mainly because no convicts were transported there. Plus, the opal fields were attracting a lot of fortune hunters and people looking to start a new life, as was the case of our granduncle,' he informed them.

Vince jumped in. 'This is getting out of hand. Trying to locate Meris's family is one thing, which will be hard enough, seeing as we don't have much information. At least they travelled sometime in the seventies, but our granduncle would have immigrated sometime at the beginning of the century. I don't imagine there would be much information from that time.'

Chaz shrugged his shoulders. 'Good luck trying to convince our mother that it could be a wild goose chase! You know, when she gets her mind set on something, there is no talking her out of it.'

'So, what do we know about this place, Adelaide? Because it looks to me like we will be heading in that direction soon.' He turned to his brothers, and said, 'Looks like someone will have to do some research.'

Before they could protest, he jumped in. 'I'll toss you for it!'

# 2

## COOBER PEDY, 1972

'What do we do now?' Monica asked Felipe, the only one with knowledge about this weird place.

The look on his face did not inspire confidence. Fumbling in his pouch, he pulled out some crumpled papers. Searching through them, he extracted a card. 'This is the contact I was given by the fellow that helped us get out here,' waving it as if that solved everything.

'What does it say?' she asked.

He turned it over and began to read, 'It says he will be in this pub every day from about noon, the instructions say to come there when we arrive, and he will help with getting set up.'

Monica could see his hesitation, 'So who is this guy, and what's in it for him?'

A worried look crossed his face. 'Like I told you guys in the beginning, I met this guy who came back from here after hitting it rich with opal. He said there was a fortune to be made, that opal was everywhere. This guy gave me this contact; he said he makes his living by helping people get started. That's all I know.'

Diego cut in, 'Okay, enough talk, we are here, so let's try to make the best of it. What's the name of the place we are to meet?'

'Its name is "Digeridoos",' Felipe replied.

'And there it is!' cried Rosa, pointing to a dugout entrance on the opposite side of the street with the name emblazoned on the fence.

They trudged across, dragging their meagre belongings with them. As they entered, they were taken by the immediate change in temperature. Inside it was cool and dry. Oil lamps provided the lighting, and a window set high on the front wall provided a yellowish glow.

Monica went to the bar, now designated talker due to her better command of English. She ordered drinks and then turned to Felipe, 'What's this fellow's name again?' she asked. He gave her the name, and turning to the bar lady, she asked, 'We are looking for a chap called George Pratt. We are told he comes in here every day.'

The woman's attitude changed at once. 'You are not from around these parts, are you?

Monica nodded. 'No, we are from Spain and have immigrated here.'

'And let me guess, someone told you could come here and make your fortune digging for opals,' with a grin on her face.

Monica nodded. The woman slid the drinks across to her. 'Here, these are on the house. They come with some advice, which I am sure you will disregard, but here goes. Take the drinks, enjoy them, and then get out of this hell hole as fast as possible. If you decide to stay, Georgie will be in any time soon, but be careful. This is a dangerous place. With many warring factions. Do not trust anyone, and guard your valuables.'

Monica was visibly shocked. 'So, it is not true that there are opals here?'

The woman laughed again. 'No, my dear, there are plenty of opals. The problem is that it is buried under tons of rock and dirt. Believe me, if it was easy to find them, do you think I would be serving bar in a cave'?

Monica brought the drinks to the table where her friends were sitting. The expression on her face snapped them to attention.

'What's wrong?' Diego asked.

She went on the explain what the woman had said. Felipe mocked her. 'Of course, they would say they want to keep it all for themselves, I bet!' and grabbing his drink.

'Well, if they are making so much money, how come this place looks like this? I don't see anybody swanning about in fancy cars, and where are the Mansions'?' Diego asked.

They lapsed into silence, each lost in their thoughts until a greasy-looking guy with thick black hair came in and made his way to the bar sometime later. When his drink arrived, he spoke to the woman behind the bar, who pointed to the sad-looking bunch sitting at the table. He made his way over, pulled up a chair, and sat down.

'Hear you guys are looking for me? Georgie is the name, and at your service,' he announced, handshakes all around.

Monica decided to take charge. 'My friend was given your name by someone that said you would be able to get us set up here.' Turning to Felipe for more information, 'What was he called?' she asked.

He fumbled in his clutter of papers again, 'His name is Mick Tucker. He says he was from here, made his fortune, and decided to see the world. He said you were the man to see to get started.' Monica translated as the confused expression on the guy's face told her he had not got a word of it.

'Mick Tucker, I wondered what happened to him. He told you he made his fortune, did he?' He laughed. 'Well, anything is possible, but the last time I saw him, he was high tailing it out of town with a posse on his tail. He was one of the 'Nightshift' and was caught in the act and lucky to get away with his life.'

Confused, she asked, 'Nightshift?'

'Yes, he replied, 'that's what they called claim jumpers. They would go to a claim after dark while the miner was sleeping and see if they could benefit from all their work during the day. The problem is not if there is opal, it is the amount of earth that has to be moved to find it, plus most have to be done by hand. It is backbreaking work. Did he get any money from you?' he asked.

They turned to Felipe for a reply. He again got a sheepish look on his face. 'No, he only sold me his claim. He said he had all he needed for life and sold it to us at a bargain price.'

The look on Rosa's face told them this was news to her.

George burst out laughing, yelling across to the bar. 'Shelia, Mick Tucker sold these poor souls his claim, told them he had all he needed from it.'

She and the few patrons in the bar burst out laughing. 'What's so funny?' Felipe asked, his face reddening. 'Son, a claim is wherever you start digging a hole. Just don't dig where someone else is digging. If they leave, it is fair game. What did you pay him for his claim?' George asked, with a grin on his face.

Felipe jumped up, flushed with anger. '*Voy a bano,*' he snapped, marching off.

'He is going to the toilet,' Rosa informed them.

'Probably to shit himself,' George roared, much to the crowd's delight.

They drowned their sorrows with a drink for a couple of hours, then arranged to meet George in the morning to see about getting set up.

'You will need somewhere to sleep tonight,' he informed them. 'Try the Bedrock Underground Inn. It is just next door. I will pick you up there tomorrow,' leaving them to get settled in their new nightmare.

# 3

## MALLORCA

Summer was drawing to its close, and like flicking a switch, the Island dropped into hibernation. Most of the bars and clubs closed, and those that remained open, such as their local 'Blue Bar,' mainly catered to the locals.

The Heart family had a bar and restaurant outside Magaluf, but they were not reliant on it for income due to Bill's various 'business interests' and so it was closed during the week. Hence, they were all having dinner in the Blue Bar that late summer evening and the conversation returned to the search for Meris's sister and husband.

'We have very little to go on. Even with the help of Chaz's girlfriend, the wonderful *Christine de la Vega,* who has put her considerable resources to try and locate them, we still only know when they arrived in Adelaide and were granted immigrant status,' Bill declared.

Meris was not having a bar of it. 'Charlie, surely you can use your influence to get your lady to put some pressure on the authorities over there for more information,' she pleaded.

'First of all, you lot, she is not my girlfriend. At best I am some light entertainment for her, but I am seeing her this weekend, and she said she has some information for us. But before you get excited, she has said it may not be of any help.'

Ever since the brothers discovered some lost Nazi treasure and figured out a way for her to use it to her best advantage, they had become the darlings of the establishment. And in the case of Chaz, the *Gobernadora* had taken a shine to him, making him the toast of the island and the most significant talking point amongst the gossipers. Something he was not happy about. Much as he liked her company, he was not fond of the flash parties and all the unwanted attention.

Meris yelped in delight. 'At last, we may be able to begin the search,' she cried.

'Don't get your hopes up yet. She had tried many times before and came up empty-handed,' he cautioned.

But Meris was not to be deterred. 'I have a good feeling this time,' which prompted groans from the table.

'Drink up, everybody. I reckon we are off again!' Des roared as he raised his glass.

# 4

## COOBER PEDY

The following day after a restless night in their unfamiliar surroundings, they all met at Digeridoos Bar and Grill for their meeting with the mysterious George character. Monica nudged Diego at the appearance of a very sheepish Filipe, followed by an even more worried-looking Rosa.

After they had booked their accommodation the night before, Monica immediately got stuck with him. 'You never told us that you paid that character back home for a claim. Did you use the money we lent you?' she asked.

Diego had foolishly told him how they had stumbled upon a lost treasure back in Mallorca. They had taken only a few precious stones to give them a fresh start. They had sold enough to pay for the trip and lent their friends some to help them pay for their trip.

Felipe became very uncomfortable. 'I paid him from our savings,' he blustered.

Something judging by the expression on Rosa's face, he had neglected to inform her. Before they could continue the conversation, George came through the door. As he approached, Diego grabbed Felipe by the collar and pulled him close, whispering, 'Whatever happens, you don't mention the diamonds,' pushing him away as his friend approached.

'How are you this morning? Slept well in your new underground digs?'

Diego answered. 'We grew up underground back home, so we are used to it,' pointing at his wife.

That surprised George. 'So, you have experience in mining?' he asked. Diego ignored him. 'So, what's the plan?'

'Straight to business, I like that. Well, first you will need transport. You can buy a Ute from the car yard here, it will be more expensive than back in Adelaide, but everything is here, as transport costs,' he added.

'What's a Ute'?' Monica asked.

He laughed, 'Easier if I show you. Let's grab some breakfast so we can get started. Back in a minute, just hitting the bog.' The confused look on their faces made him laugh. 'Toilet,' he said, pointing at the bathrooms.

As soon as he left, Diego turned to Felipe, 'What is the story with this guy? Why is he helping us? What have you promised him?'

Again, he avoided eye contact. 'Nothing, only that we would cut him in on any find we make. The guy back home told me how it is done over here,' he protested.

'Well, from this point on, don't make any promises on our behalf before discussing it with us,' pointing at his wife.

Before Felipe could respond, Georgie returned, 'I hope you don't mind, but I ordered a full breakfast for everybody. It would help if you had a good feed in the morning here. Not much to eat out in the desert unless you like eating snakes!' he sniggered.

Before Diego could respond, Monica interjected. 'That's fine, but we will order our food in the future. We have a different eating styles.'

He shrugged his shoulders. 'Whatever blows your skirt up, only trying to help,' as he glanced at Felipe.

After breakfast, which they had to agree was just what they needed after the last couple of harrowing days, they searched for transport.

At the car yard, George pointed to one of the vehicles. 'That is a Ute.'

It looked to them like a cross between a car and an open truck. 'Look, it even has four seats in the front. It's perfect,' yelped Rosa as they all proceeded to inspect this new vehicle.

The owner wandered over, and George rushed in quickly to do the introductions. 'This is Steve. He owns this establishment,' as he introduced his friends.

The guy ignored George, something that did not go unnoticed by Diego. 'I see that this type of vehicle is new to you. It was conceived here in Australia because, as you can see as well as transport, it makes a perfect work vehicle. Let me guess, you are new around these parts?

Monica responded by filling him in on where they were from and what had brought them here.

He continued. 'Well, you guys sure are brave, this place is not for the faint-hearted, and I am sure you are concerned about what is in store for you. As far as my establishment is concerned, you are entirely secure, I am the only one that sells vehicles here, and because of that, I guarantee all sales. I would not last long here if I sold duds.'

Again, a confused look crossed Monica's face. He nodded. 'Sorry, you will have to get used to Aussie slang. 'Dud' is no good,' he said as he glanced at George. 'Come on, and I will give you a test drive.'

Monica looked at Diego, then said to Steve, 'No need, we will take it.'

He looked surprised. 'That's something that doesn't happen every day.'

She looked him square in the eye. 'We are completely out of our depth here in this strange country and this even stranger place and are vulnerable to being taken advantage of, so my husband and I have decided to follow our instincts, and mine is that I trust you, so whatever we pay and receive is up to you.'

'Wow, lady, you drive a hard bargain. You put me in a position where I have to go the extra mile for you. Come on down to my office,' pointing to an entrance cut into the cliff face.

They emerged two hours later, the proud owner of a Holden Ute. Steve had also thrown in all the necessary digging equipment as the guy who owned the Ute had left it behind as he abandoned his dream of riches.

As they were leaving, Steve pulled Diego aside. 'Be careful of George, he runs with the wrong crowd. If you need to chat to somebody, I have a friendly ear.'

They shook hands and agreed to catch up, as he stepped out into his new life.

# 5

**CHARLIE.**
**DUBLIN, PRESENT DAY**

Call it homesick if you like, but I needed a break from all the glamour and excitement of life down in Mallorca. Plus, my relationship with the lovely *Christine de la Vaga*, although very enjoyable, her lifestyle was as far removed from mine as you could get. I just needed to sit down in my local pub and share some stories with my mates over a few pints, to reconnect with my former life.

But that was to be short-lived. I had no sooner arrived home, and my mother was on me like white on rice.

'I have great news. Your cousin has discovered some exciting information about your granduncle. He had discovered where he found work when he arrived in Adelaide,' she declared excitedly.

I groaned under my breath. I had hoped she would have forgotten about this wild goose chase, but since the search for her new friend Meris's lost sister, they had been in continuous contact, comparing notes. Before I could mount an objection, she jumped in again.

'I have just got off the phone with her, and she tells me they are expecting some positive news about the search from your girlfriend. This could be just the news we have been waiting for.'

'First of all, she is not my girlfriend, she is the Governor of the Balearic Islands, and I am one of the help,' I cried in desperation.

I could see where this was heading, and the last place I wanted to go was off to some far-off land in search of an uncle that had the good sense to leave during those troubled times.

'I knew you would screw that good thing up after all the good work I put in on your behalf,' my dad grumbled from over at the fireplace where he was sitting with his newspaper and a whiskey.

I ignored him, continuing the conversation with my mother. 'Ma, you must realise that Australia is vast, as big as the United States. It would be like looking for a needle in a haystack,' I pleaded. That is when she played her winning hand.

'Fine, I suppose I will have to ask Meris if her family will help. Desmond has already agreed to help search for their poor lost souls. Terrible when you can't even count on your own family in your old age.' Her voice broke into a weak cackle.

'Well played, Ma, okay, where is this new information?'

Without hesitation, she produced some handwritten notes, handing them to me. Reading them, I quickly discovered that the 'exciting news' was that they had discovered that they had moved to Melbourne, where he had got employment in an amusement park called Lunar Park.

'This is it, nothing more?' I asked.

Her excitement was not to be dampened. 'Look what you were able to do with Desmond's little problem. This will be easy for you.'

I was dumbfounded. Des's little problem had resulted in the sinking of a luxury yacht, numerous gang wars, and the discovery of lost treasure!

Before I could respond, Dad interjected. 'You would think by now you are wasting your time. When your mother, and more importantly, your grandmother, gets an idea in their head, the game is over.'

I nodded in resignation. 'I am going for a drink, interested?' I asked him, as we headed for the door.

He was out of his chair like a shot. My mother cried, 'Hold on, you are not leaving me out,' as she grabbed her coat.

# 6

## MALLORCA

As Chaz collected his luggage and made his way out of the terminal, he found Christine waiting for him with her limo and driver, to his surprise.

'Charles!' she cried, giving him a big hug and a fashionable kiss on both cheeks, much to his discomfort.

'I did not expect to see you here?' he stammered.

'I just had to meet you. I have news for you regarding your missing relations.'

He did not bother to point out that he was not related, only a family friend.

'Come, let's go. I told the Hearts I had some information to share,' as she ushered him into the back of the Limo.

As they headed to the Hearts ranch, he noticed she had become silent. 'So, what's this news, that's so important?' he asked.

Concerned crossed her face. 'That's why I waited until your return, the news is not all good, and I wanted you here when I shared it.'

He was confused. 'Why? I am sure they are hanging out for any information.'

Again, she avoided eye contact. 'Charles, my observation is that whenever your family, and your friends, encounter difficulties, they turn to you. I believe this news will require your assistance,' as she settled in her seat, indicating that he would have to wait until they were all gathered.

The Hearts family had assembled at the pool area when they arrived and greetings were made. They clamoured for whatever news they had.

Christine put her hand up. 'I decided to come personally with what my people have discovered about your sister,' nodding to Meris. 'However, the news is not all positive.'

Before they could interrupt, Chaz spoke, 'Why don't we allow Christine to finish? Then perhaps she can answer questions,' indicating for her to continue.

She nodded gratefully. 'I know this is so difficult for you, be assured we have done all possible from this end. We have discovered what ship they sailed on,' consulting a notebook she held. 'It was the HMS *Australis*, and they were granted entry to the port of Adelaide. You should know they were registered as man and wife. From there, they purchased tickets to a place called Coober Pedy, famous for opals, and many immigrants went there chasing their fortune. From what little information we could access to all accounts, they settled in and had begun to mine for opal. That was until six months after their arrival. There was an incident.'

She paused to compose herself. 'This is where it gets difficult because the community there is very secretive, and the information we received was very hazy, so please bear with me. The report we received states that Diego was involved in an altercation with a shady character called George Pratt, which involved him giving this George fellow a severe beating.' She paused again. 'It goes on to say that George Pratt was discovered later that night beside the Suarez's claim, dead!'

There was a gasp from the family. Finally, it was Bill that spoke. 'So how does this involve Diego and Monica?' he asked.

Christine put the notebook down and looked straight at them. 'That's just it. We don't know because they vanished that night and have not been seen since!'

# 7

## COOBER PEDY
## SIX MONTHS AFTER ARRIVAL

Diego and Felipe climbed from the Ute, exhausted after another long day at their claim with the same disappointing results they had since they commenced six months ago. It had started with enthusiasm, but the daily grind of digging and sieving tons of rock with minimal rewards had worn them down.

They made their way into the pub, where Diego was greeted by an expectant smile from his wife Monica, who had got work behind the bar, and Rosa in the kitchen. He dropped his head, shaking it grimly. She just shrugged her shoulders, nodding in the resignation of their predicament.

It had started like that as soon as they discovered there was no value to the so-called claim rights Felipe had purchased. George Pratt had informed them that they had to pick out a piece of desert, register it with the land office, and they were away. When they asked how you knew where the best place would be to stake a claim, he laughed, waving in all directions.

'Opal is everywhere around here. The sixty-four-thousand-dollar question is where the opal is. It is just up to chance, so pick a spot and dig'.

So that's what they did. But after relocating their claim a couple of times, with little success, their patience was running out, especially Felipe, who was not fond of the backbreaking work.

They made their way to the bar. By this time, they had adopted the customs of this barren area and had let their hair grow out and grown bushy beards, so much so that as far as the locals were concerned, they looked identical, mainly because of their Spanish complexion and black hair. Even Monica had to take a second glance as they sat down.

As she put their drinks in front of them, taking their money, she asked, 'No luck again?'

It was Felipe who responded. 'This place is a curse. We must have moved enough dirt to fill the Grand Canyon, for we have only collected enough opal in six months to pay for fuel. If the girls were not working, we could not even cover our expenses.'

Diego took a giant slug of his beer. 'If it were easy, everybody that comes here would be rich. From what I can see, the only ones that seem to make it here are those that are in for the long haul. Remember, this was your idea. We are here now and might as well give it our best shot.'

Felipe dropped his head, mumbling, 'Perhaps we should head to that place George spoke about, Lighting Creek, where the most valuable opal is found, the black opal.'

'That is in NSW, which is on the other side of the country, it would cost a fortune to relocate there, with no more chance of success than here. Anyway, how would we pay for it?' Diego asked.

Felipe turned his head and slyly replied. 'You still have some diamonds left, don't you?'

Diego grabbed him by the arm, dragging him close, 'Are you crazy, mentioning that in here, there are plenty around that will kill you for a few bits of opal? What do you think they would do for a few diamonds, idiot? Keep your mouth shut. In any case, those are the only things

Monica and I have to fall back on. Don't mention it again,' shoving him away in disgust.

The creak of the pub door opening caused him to glance over his shoulder and to add fuel to the fire. It was George.

Over the last couple of months, he and Monica had developed a friendship with the friendly car dealer Steve Yakov. He had filled them on the running of this strange place. He had warned them not to trust anyone, as the law had little control over their lawlessness. 'There are a couple of fractions at work here. First, you have my mob, the Croats and the Serbs. If they are not fighting, they organise all the criminal activities around here.'

'But you are a Serb. Do they give you any trouble?' Monica had asked.

He smiled. 'I was here first, my town my rules, let's leave it at that,' as he continued with his story. 'The other group to watch out for is the 'Nightshift',' and before they could respond, he continued. 'They are thieves that befriend newcomers and 'help' them set up. Then if they succeed, they come at night and work the claim while you are asleep.'

'Is there nothing that can be done?' Diego asked.

Steve nodded. 'Many take the matter into their own hands.'

They looked at him with a quizzical 'how?'

'One method is to pour petrol down the shaft and set them on fire or drop a bit of gelignite down. The explosion leaves the deaf with headaches for a long time! I tell you this because that George fella is one of that crew, so don't trust him.'

They exchanged glances. 'He has nothing to do with us, he is Felipe's friend,' Monica said.

Steve shrugged. 'That remains to be seen.'

# 8

Diego snapped back to the present when he felt George's presence. 'How did we go today, boys?' he asked, clapping Felipe on the back.

'No good, just a few fragments, still chasing that elusive strike,' he grumbled.

George's attitude changed at once. 'Boys, my investment in time and effort in our little venture has shown me precious little return so far. May I suggest you put in a bit more effort, perhaps invest in some digging equipment to speed things up? I would hate to withdraw my support. I can't imagine how you would survive in this outback place without my assistance.'

Before any could respond, Diego was on his feet, gripping George by the throat, lifting him with ease, slamming him down across a table. The crowd stood back in dismay and amazement. This guy had a bad reputation and ran with the 'Nightshift', not someone to be messed with. So, to see him being maltreated like a little child brought a look of satisfaction to a lot of the assembled onlookers.

As he struggled to breathe, Diego snarled loudly in his ear, so all could hear. 'Listen to me carefully, you little worm, whatever arrangement you have with him,' pointing at Felipe, who was in shock at the bar, 'is his business. As far as my wife and I are concerned, we have never had anything to do with you, so stay away from us. If you persist, we will have words.'

He released George from his grip, who proceeded to massage his neck. Then he made the mistake of taking it further.

'Some friend you are, carrying around a fortune in diamonds, and you won't even buy equipment to help your friends out,' he croaked.

Like a dam breaking, all the frustrations and the betrayal of his so-called friend for revealing the existence of their nest egg all came to a head. He launched himself at George, smashing him with a massive punch, beating him until his wife's cry brought him to his senses. He dragged George to his feet, propelling him to the door, and flung him like a sack of rubbish into the middle of the road.

'Don't ever mention my family or anything connected to us again, or this will not be over!' he warned.

As he closed the door, the threats and curses could be heard, 'You have not heard the last of this, you foreign prick. You will get yours.'

Diego ignored him as the shouts receded and George headed off to lick his wounds.

'Have you gone mad? He will bring his gang after us now,' Felipe snapped.

Before he could continue, Diego grabbed him. 'Shut up! You are the cause of all this. You decided to use this guy, not us,' indicating his wife. 'You have put us all in danger thanks to your big mouth.'

Felipe began to bluster. 'If you had not been so tight with your stash, we could have bought the machinery to dig faster.'

'You idiot, first of all, that nest egg is for Monica and me in case this venture doesn't work out. But thanks to you, we now know the answer. I don't know what your plans are, but from tomorrow, we are on our own.' Slamming down his drink, he headed for the door.

'Where are you going?' Monica asked.

'Just going to take care of something,' as he vanished outside.

\* \* \*

It was just after dawn when the commotion outside woke them. Monica and Diego went to the window to see what was going on. There was a crowd gathered, and they could hear one of the miners talking loudly. What they heard shocked them to the core.

'George is dead. I found him by the foreigner's claim. His head is bashed in. It looks like the Diego guy finished the job.'

'You can't say that for sure. Let's ask him,' an old digger said.

The guy shrugged his shoulders. 'Don't see how. All the equipment is gone from the claim, along with their Ute.

'Has anybody checked their rooms?' another digger asked.

The crowd headed for where the couple were staying. One of the diggers cried out, 'There's his partner. Let's ask him.'

Rushing over to question him, 'Have you seen your pal, Diego?' one of them asked.

Filipe stood dumbfounded, shaking his head.

'You are wasting your time,' the old digger growled from the back. 'Their Ute and all their equipment is gone. There are only two directions they could go, north or south, you pick. But Diego is gone!'

# 9

## BARCELONA AIRPORT
## PRESENT DAY

Things moved pretty fast after the visit from Christine.

Meris nor Maria could be dissuaded from immediately mounting a search. We all quickly realised that nothing would change their minds. We couldn't even play the poverty card, thanks to Des providing us with a big windfall from his treasure adventure. So, it was decided that Des and Maria would travel to Australia to discover what had happened to Diego and Monica.

Vince, our brother, the legal mastermind of our family, and Bill, Meris's husband, were in London, sorting out one of their many business deals and counting themselves out of what they believed would be a futile venture.

Which left Chaz, who could see he had run out of excuses for not going on his search for his mother's long-lost granduncle. So it was, he found himself with Des and Maria in the business lounge at Barcelona airport, awaiting their long flight with United Emirates to Australia. They had decided to travel together to Adelaide, get over their jetlag, and get accustomed to their new surroundings. Chaz wanted to start in Melbourne, as this was his only starting point. But as usual, Des decided in his usual way by 'tossing for it'.

Thus they were headed for Adelaide!

# 10

After they cleared immigration and customs, they grabbed their luggage and caught a taxi to the city centre, which was only a short hop from the airport.

They had reserved rooms in the exclusive Eos by SkyCity on the river. After checking in, they decided to clean up after the long journey and meet back in the lobby to take a stroll and check out the sights.

Not far from the hotel was The Central Market. It surprised them that although things seemed much the same as markets in Europe, the fruit and produce, especially the fish, were very different. As they exited the market, Maria gave an excited cry, 'Look, a Spanish restaurant,' pointing to place across the street. 'San Churro.'

They took a table outside. The waiter soon arrived with menus, and Maria began speaking in Spanish. The young man broke into a huge smile, signalling to an older gent behind the counter. When he approached, they quickly descended into rapid-fire Spanish.

Finally, Maria turned to the brothers. 'This is Rick and Blanco. Blanco is his dad. Can I let them choose dinner for us?'

The boys nodded, leaving Maria to her chat. 'Well, since you are the expert on this place, what have you found out about this Coober Ped place?' Chaz asked.

Des took a sip of sangria, and said, 'Okay, from what I could find out, it would seem that it and the moon would have a lot in common. It can reach 50 degrees Celsius at the height of the day. So, as I told you before, many people live underground. It is not a place for the faint-hearted.'

'Sounds wonderful,' Chas retorted.

'I guess the chance of riches will drive some people to give anything a go. It makes you wonder what type of people Diego and Monica were.'

'Are,' Monica interjected. 'You said "were". I believe they could still be alive,' she mumbled, tears in her eyes.

Des put his arm around her. 'Sorry, we did not mean that. Of course they could be alive, and hopefully we can find out more soon. So let's celebrate our first night here in Adelaide.'

# 11

After a perfect night in this top hotel, the following morning at breakfast, feeling reinvigorated as they ate out on the balcony. The weather was perfect, about 24 degrees Celsius. It was early summer, and a balmy wind caressed their faces as we relaxed with a coffee.

'What would our next move be?' Des asked.

It was Chaz who, as usual, was the one with a plan. 'Well, the first thing we should do is check how the search for them is going.'

Maria looked confused. 'How can we do that?' she asked.

'Well, if he they under suspicion in the death of that guy, the police would have a file on them. I think that's where we should start.'

Finishing up, they went to reception to enquire where police headquarters were. The receptionist smiled. 'You're in luck. It is in walking distance. Just a couple of blocks, in Angus Street.'

When they arrived, Chaz was immediately impressed with how the building looked. It was beautifully presented, and when they went to the counter, they were greeted as if they were there to purchase a new car. He had never encountered anything like this in his relationship with the police in any other country.

'How can we help you, sir?' asked a police officer, a sergeant.

'We are from Ireland and Spain,' he explained, 'looking for a long-lost relative,' and gave the officer a condensed version of the story.

The sergeant gasped. 'Well, that's quite a story. The person you need to speak to would be from the major crimes squad. Let me see if I can get somebody for you. Take a seat over there, and we will contact you to take care of it as soon as possible.'

As they went over to the couch to wait, Des whispered, 'Are you sure this is a police station? It is more like a hotel.'

A minute later, a solid-looking guy appeared at the top of the stairs. As he descended, the aura of confidence that exuded from him was apparent. His body language screamed, 'I am someone with whom you did not mess!'

He approached, extending his hand. Again, something only sometimes happened with police forces they had previously encountered.

'Chief Inspector David George at your service,' shaking their hands in turn.

Chaz took the lead and began to tell him the story again, but before he had got a few words out, the chief inspector interrupted him. 'I would love to hear your story. Let's go to my office where I have access to my computer, so I can follow up as we talk?'

Nodding in agreement, they went to his spacious office. Charlie just had to ask, 'I hope you don't mind, but we are in wonder of your headquarters and the attention we have received. Where we come from, if this were happening, we would be hollering for a lawyer,' he joked, but he was unsure if he had gone too far.

The chief inspector laughed. 'No worries. To be honest, I was in earshot when they got the call about your inquiries, and I heard mention of where you guys are from. I decided to check you out for myself. I have Scottish blood in my family. And my wife is half-Spanish. You can guess my curiosity. So, let's hear your story.'

When Chaz had finished with his tale, the guy had not said a word, just clicked away at his computer. Finally, he looked up, a puzzled look on his face. 'Well, I had their entry in Adelaide Port back in 1972, but after that, nothing. Here is what I suggest. There is a hotel across the road called The Seven Stars. If you head over there, you can grab a bite to eat, and I will join you when I investigate this a bit more.'

It was just about lunchtime, and they gladly agreed, delighted to be getting this much help. Glancing at his watch, the chief inspector added, 'Shouldn't be too long. I am just going to make a few phone calls. Sometimes the old methods are the best,' giving the boys a knowing look that gave them shivers.

# 12

Making their way across to the pub, Des spoke first. 'Would not like to get on the wrong side of that fellow,' he remarked.

It was Maria who responded. 'Something you should try to remember when you are talking to him,' she warned.

They had just finished their lunch when the massive figure of Chief Inspector David George appeared beside their table, signalling to the guy behind the bar, who knew exactly what he wanted. Pulling a chair over, he plopped down like an old buddy. 'They treating you okay? Was the food up to scratch?'

'All good, could not be better,' Des quickly assured him.

The chief inspector's drink arrived, and he began his story. He explained that he had rung an old pal from the force. 'This guy had been in charge of the station at Port Augusta. They handled all the problems from Coober Pedy back then and surprisingly remembered the case.' He paused to take a drink.

Des used the opportunity to jump in, much to the disgust of the others. 'Did he know our friends?'

The chief inspector continued as if he had not heard a word. 'No, it was mainly because of what happened. They were called the morning after the 'incident.' When he arrived later that day, everybody had gone to the ground.' He could see their puzzled faces, so he began to explain. 'Coober Pedy is where many people go to disappear, so as you can imagine, it was not easy to get people to talk. All he could discover was that some local thug had got into a fight with your friend, Diego, and the next day the guy was discovered with his head bashed in, and your friends had disappeared. So, my pal issued a search bulletin to bring them in for questioning.'

Again, Des could not help himself. 'Did they have any luck?'

This time he responded. 'That's where it gets strange. My guy gets word from above to close the search down and put it down as unsolved, which is not unusual with cases in that place. They tended to take care of their problems.' He paused to let them digest this new information.

'Who shut the investigation down?' Des asked.

The chief inspector glanced around, then said, 'I shouldn't tell you this, but it was long ago. He told me it was the anti-terrorist unit. In the past, I have been connected with them. I called one of my contacts and made some discrete inquiries. She returned quickly and said to drop it, telling me it was connected to an ongoing investigation. All I could get was that it involved the Serbs and other eastern European groups, who are involved in crime at all levels, including dealing with terrorist groups.'

'So, all search for them has stopped?' Maria asked.

He nodded, 'As far as I can see, the matter is closed; the death of that guy was dropped. Therefore, all interest in your friends stopped. Remember, that place is where people usually go to disappear, so no surprise there was no follow-up. Sorry I couldn't be of more help.'

Chaz jumped in, 'You have been a great help. Before we spoke to you, we had practically no information.'

'So, what for you guys now?' he asked.

Chaz replied. 'Well, not sure about these guys,' indicting Maria and his brother. 'But I have a quest of my own,' as he explained his search for their grandmother's brother's possible family.

The chief inspector roared with laughter and surprise. 'It's true, you Irish are mad, and it seems that the Spanish are not far behind them. At least you are heading to a more civilised part of the country. You will enjoy your time in Melbourne. If you need any more assistance, here is my number. Feel free to give me a call,' and held out a card.

Taking it, Chaz said, 'We can't thank you enough.'

The chief inspector stood, finished his drink, and then shook their hands, wishing them luck. As he gripped Chaz's hand, he whispered, 'Keep that number safe. If I sense the type of guy you are. and what you will encounter in this country, I feel you will need it.'

He strode off and gave him a solid slap on his back. Chaz felt a cold shiver run down his spine at his warning.

'What did he say'?' Des asked.

'Nothing, just wishing me luck,' he replied, hoping he would not need it.

# 13

The following morning they were at the airport again. They had spent last evening back at the Spanish restaurant on the insistence of Maria. Discussing their options late into the night, they had decided on a plan. Chaz would fly to Melbourne to follow up on his slender lead, and Des and Maria would fly to Coober Pedy, hoping to find something to bring closure to the family.

They had discovered that flights to Coober Pedy were for the next day, so they charted a small plane to take them. At the same time, Chaz had bought a ticket for Melbourne. He was leaving about an hour before Des and Marie's plane would be ready.

They walked him to his gate when his flight was called, agreeing to speak that night when they were set.

Shortly after he left, Des and Maria were called to a private lounge to await their flight. As they were sipping champagne, Des remarked. 'I wonder if your aunt could see us now, considering the hardship it must have been for them.' He clinked glasses with Maria. 'Here's to them, wherever they are.'

Shortly after, they were escorted to their plane, a Cessna six-seater turboprop. As soon as they wear airborne, the steward presented a selection of small but delicious snacks. Maria asked him how long the flight would be.

'Just under two hours should have you on the ground. A car will be waiting to take you to your hotel directly,' he replied. 'Meanwhile, enjoy the view. You will fly over some of the most spectacular landscapes on the planet. That is not my quote,' he quickly added, 'it is the opinion of most travel writers,' leaving them to get their first glimpse of the outback.

The landing was as smooth as the flight, and as they taxied towards a private terminal at the corner of the airport, they began looking around at the barren landscape. Des was the first to comment. 'We must be a long way from the city, can't see much building activity around here.'

The attendant laughed. 'Sadly, it's only four kilometres away. Everything looks a bit like this around here. That's why almost all of the city is underground.' With that, he pushed open the aircraft door, and the blast of hot air that engulfed them almost took their breath away. 'Now you know why they live underground!'

They made a dash for the car that was waiting at the bottom of the steps. As they stepped in, the door closed and the blast of cold air was heavenly. 'How does anybody survive with this heat?' Des asked the driver, who chuckled, and without turning, replied, 'She's not a bad one today. You would not want to be here on a hot one, mate!'

The car roared off in a cloud of dust. Within minutes, they pulled up to the entrance of The Desert Cave Motel. 'Head inside and follow the signs to reception. They will look after you. Don't worry about your bags. We will take care of them,' the cheery driver said.

Inside they were greeted by a sign inviting them to take the lift to reception on the bottom floor. Stepping in, they could see there were four levels. 'I read about this. They have discovered a use for a lot of the former diggings, converting them into homes and hotels. There is even a shopping mall underground,' Des explained.

Stepping out, they looked in amazement. It was like a buzzing city centre mall. They were surrounded by shops of all descriptions that mainly catered to tourists.

'Over here,' Maria said, pointing towards the hotel reception, which was situated in front of what appeared to be a bar and restaurant.

'Hello, welcome to the Desert Cave, first time underground?' the young receptionist asked.

'Where we come from, they usually leave that for the dead people,' Des replied.

The girl was silent for a minute, then burst into laughter, 'You Irish, always with a joke. You must be Desmond and Maria Savage. We received all your information and requests from your hotel in Adelaide.'

Des grinned, 'Actually, we are not married,' he said as he signed the registrar.

The girl giggled as she replied. 'We don't worry about such thing around here. Lord knows if we did, I don't believe we would have many guests,' giving Maria a big smile. 'As for that other information you were seeking. Our manager reached out to his old colleagues, who suggested the best place for you to start would be the Bedrock Underground Inn. I hope that is of help.'

Des thanked her. Before they left Adelaide, he had got the manager at the hotel to reach out and see if they could help locate a favourite drinking spot for the locals around the 70s. 'Is it far from here?' he asked.

'Just across the road, when you go to your room on the top floor, still underground,' she quickly added. 'But because you are close to the surface, you have natural light from a tunnel shaft.'

Thanking her, they headed up again to locate their room. It was surprisingly regular in appearance, except for the earthen walls. As well as the background lighting, they had sunshine beaming from the shaft.

'Look, you can shut the sun off,' Maria said, pressing a button that sealed the skylight.

Des jumped up. 'I don't know about you, but I could not take much of this place. Let's check out this bar and see if we can get any clues.' As they were about to go, he gripped her and gave her a big hug. 'Remember, this is a very long shot. We will do our best, but please don't get your hopes up too much.'

She leaned in, giving him a peck on the cheek. 'I am not worried. You guys always come through,' leaving him with a feeling of dread.

# 14

## CHAZ, TULLAMARINE AIRPORT
## MELBOURNE

I collected my bag from the carousel when I heard my phone alert me to a message from Des that they had landed in Coober Pedy. As I made my way out to my waiting car, I flicked a quick reply that I had also just arrived in Melbourne.

I had decided, regardless of the outcome of this adventure, that I would enjoy the journey. For the first time in my life, I could really indulge myself, mostly thanks to Des's efforts and a tidy windfall that had left us very flush.

I arrived at the Luxury St Kilda Townhouse, which was pretty much the whole top floor of the building. I should add, in my defence, that I had asked for it to be within walking distance of Luna Park, and it ticked that box. It was less than five minutes away!

After checking out my palatial dwellings, as it was early afternoon, I decided to take a stroll to look at Luna Park. True to their word, it was only a short walk to the site. The entrance was a gaping clown's mouth, which sent shivers up my spine. I never fancied the whole clown thing, not really trusting the whole idea of old geezers dressing up for kids party's. I bought an entrance ticket and asked where the administration building was.

After a bit of searching, I finally found the building I was looking for. Inside, a quietly spoken lady at reception asked me if she could help. I then related my strange story and my search for my long-lost Granduncle.

'Goodness, that was a long time ago. I am not sure we would have any records from that far back.' She then explained that the place had been closed during the war, undergoing significant renovations, including a roller-coaster called the Big Dipper.

'Let me get Mister Williams. He has been here forever. If anybody can help you, it is him. He remembers this place's history,' directing me to take a seat as she searched for this guy.

Shortly after, she returned with someone who looked a little like Yoda from Star Wars. After introductions were made, he invited me back to his office. 'Take a seat, my goodness. It is a long time since anybody has inquired about this place from that era,' he mumbled.

'I understand that the chances are slim, but I promised my mother I would do my best. I told her it would be a long shot,' I replied.

He nodded. 'Well, you are talking about back at the beginning. It all started when an American showman named JD Williams, no relation,' he hastily added, 'and a couple of brothers, the Phillips, bought the defunct showground called Dreamworld. Williams had Luna Parks all over America and wanted to open over here. It was a roaring success and remained in the Philips brother's hands for years. Recently, a large transport company bought it.'

'So, do you have any records from that time?' I asked, hoping to hurry him up.

He shook his head. 'Sadly, most records were lost in the arson fires during its closed years. Over the years, there have been many efforts to reconstruct the glorious history of this old place, but details such as old employees are long gone.'

I shrugged my shoulders. 'Well, I thought it would be a long shot after all this time. Thanks for your time.'

The old gent accompanied me to the door, then stopped as something seemed to come to mind. 'Since you have come this far, and I don't want you to get your hope up, but if there is one person that would remember back to those days, it is Gavin.'

'Who'?' I asked.

'The Amazing Gavin! He was one of the early acts here. He would climb to the top of a 100-foot tower and dive into a tank of water, a real daredevil as he recalled the memory.'

My ears picked up. Any chance of bringing more information back home could only help. 'Where could I find this fellow'?' I asked.

He paused for a moment. 'Well, if he is still alive, you will find him in his favourite watering hole, The Dogs Bar, it is on Acland St,' as he gave me directions.

'How will I know him?

He laughed, 'Just ask for Gavin Lowe, or look for the oldest guy you have ever seen. Good luck in your quest, young man.'

He gave me a hearty clap on my back, sending me on my way.

# 15

I stood in front of The Dogs Bar, which looked like one of the original places that dotted this old waterfront. The sun was setting, and I figured the worst I could do was have a pleasant drink. Stepping inside, I was greeted by an atmosphere similar to one of the old pubs back in Ireland.

There was a buzzing crowd. The evening breeze drifted through, carrying the scent and sounds of the nearby sea. I found a place at the bar and ordered a pint of beer. I was just about to ask the barman if he knew this Gavin Rowe when I caught sight of a guy sitting at the end of the bar that could only be the man in question. It would be impossible to judge his age. To look at him, he looked carved out of stone and could have been anywhere between 80 and 100?

I picked up my drink and made my way over to him. 'Would I be in the company of the Amazing Gavin?' I asked.

He lifted his head, fixing me with a steely stare. 'Long time since I have been called that. Nothing amazing now. Once a fighting cock, now a feather duster, that's me. Who is asking?'

Sticking out his hand, I grasped it and was surprised by the power in his grip. 'My name is Chaz Savage, and Mr Williams from Luna Park suggested I speak to you.'

'Old Don Williams, is he still alive? My goodness, he is nearly as old as I am,' he grinned. 'And how did he think I could help you?' he asked.

'It is a long shot, but I am trying to locate some long-lost relatives; we have been told that my granduncle worked in Lun...'

'Ernie McCormack,' he cried.

I froze. 'How did you know that was who I was looking for?' I blustered.

He laughed. 'That voice and those blue eyes, you had to be a relation. You could be twins, except you are about twice the size. They must be feeding you better over there these days. Sit down, will you? You are making me dizzy looking up at you.' Pushing a stool out for me to sit, he asked, 'What are you having?'

'No, the drinks are on me,' I insisted. 'I can't believe you remember. Wait till I tell my mother.' I heard her saying, "I told you so!" as I waved to the barman for another round. 'My Grandmother was Ernie's sister. She is the one that would tell the story of his journey to the new world, along with his lady friend.'

He picked up the story. 'Sarah, that was your grandmother's name, the same as his wife. They were married on the way over by the ship's captain.' He began to tell how he and my granduncle became staunch friends. 'I was only a very you boy when I started in Lunar Park all that time ago. Ernie had been with them for some time and took me under his wing,' he explained.

The night seemed to fly by as one story blended into another. He had come out from England hoping for fame and fortune and found himself entertaining the crowds by diving from a great height into a large water tank! He went on to say that because of his fame with the wealthy clientele that flocked to make the acquaintance of somebody that was prepared to risk his life daily, he was the darling of the crowd and was able to introduce them to Ernie's exceptional talent as a boot maker. Then tragedy struck.

Sarah was pregnant with their first child and had difficulties. When she went into early childbirth, she ran into complications, and when delivering a son, she did not recover and died.

He stopped as this news hit home. 'I think it is time for something a little stronger,' I said, and called the barman over for a couple of whiskies.

As the barman poured two oversized glasses in front of us, Gavin continued his story. 'That sort of thing was common back then, and everybody back at the park chipped in to help. So, James, or Jamie as he was called, was raised by all the staff. And as soon as he was old enough, he joined the police.'

I interrupted, 'He would be retired by now. Is he still around?'

'Sadly, he was killed in the line of duty. He became a chief inspector in the major crimes squad, which dealt with the hardest criminals. He was assassinated. The word was it was eastern Europeans, but it was never solved.'

He could see the disappointment on my face. 'But he did marry a New Zealand girl, a Māori. They had a daughter. I heard she joined the police and followed her dad's path.'

'Do you know if she is still around?' I asked.

He shrugged. 'It is a long time since I even spoke about those times, but I could ask around. A lot of the old staff still keep in touch. Leave it with me, and what say you drop back in a couple of days and the worst that could happen is we continue our chat?' he said, and indicated for another round.

# 16

The Bedrock Underground Inn certainly lived up to its name. For Des, it would have fitted perfectly in an episode of The Flintstones. He half expected to see Barny Rubble sitting at the bar. He figured only the locals frequented this place, judging from the stares that greeted him and Maria as they entered. The site was hewn out of the rock with little thought to improve its appearance. The bar was a simple structure like it had been constructed out of scrap, and the woman behind the bar fitted the role perfectly. She looked like she had been cut from stone as well and, judging by the lack of a smile, was not all that happy about their presence.

'Hi,' Des said. 'We were told this was the place to come to discover all about the wonderful history of this place.'

Without looking up, the woman asked, 'Who told you that?'

Maria jumped in. 'The hotel manager back in Adelaide. We are looking for some people that immigrated here in the '70s.'

Again, without making eye contact replied with a sneer. 'Well, they wasted your time. The only thing we sell here is alcohol. So, if it is information you are looking for, you have come to the wrong place. Now, do you want something to drink?'

Des stepped in. 'Sure, give us two of your finest beers.'

When they got their drinks, they went to a table in the corner, followed by suspicious stares.

'Wow, not the friendliest place I have been in,' he whispered to Maria.

She was visibly upset. 'Why are they so mean? We are only looking for my aunt.'

'Don't forget what our friend the policeman back in Adelaide told us. This place has a law to itself. Back home, if strangers came asking questions, everybody became dumb and blind.'

It was then they heard a voice addressing them. 'I could not help overhearing you at the bar. Perhaps I can be of some help. I have been here since Adam was a boy.'

Des replied, 'We sure could do with some help. Maybe we are on a wild goose chase, but having come this far, we don't want to throw in the towel just yet. Will you join us?'

The guy glanced around, then shrugged. 'Why not? I am not that popular around here anyway.' Drawing up a chair and stuck his hand out. 'Steve Yakov, at your service, now what brings you to this godforsaken place?'

Des went on to relate the story of how on an adventure he had been on in Spain, he discovered a long-lost letter that indicated a relative thought to be dead had not perished but had immigrated here.

'Here to Coober Pedy?' he asked.

Des nodded. 'That's what somebody traced for us. They landed in Adelaide and then moved to Coober Pedy, but the trail went cold. That's why we came here, on the off chance we could locate them.'

While Des explained the story, Maria went to the bar to order more drinks. She returned with a bottle of whiskey and three glasses. As she poured a generous measure into the glasses, Steve asked, 'So, what are the names of the people you are looking for?'

Maria answered. 'Monica and Diego Suarez.'

At the sound of those names, his expression changed. Glancing around, he whispered, 'I would be better if you did not mention those names. A long time ago, those people disappeared one night without a trace. It was under a cloud of suspicion surrounding the death of a nasty piece of work called George Pratt.'

Des stepped in. 'We heard something about that from a policeman friend, but he said that the case was dropped for some reason.'

Steve shrugged. 'I don't know anything about that. I know that they vanished without a trace after the incident.' Maria began to sob as Des comforted her. Steve looked concerned. 'These people must have been significant to you.'

Maria struggled to speak. 'This was the last hope of locating my aunt. I dread telling my mother, who is convinced that Des will find them.'

Steve fixed her with a stare. 'Your aunt, I did not pick up on that she was your aunt. Are you speaking about Monica?' She nodded. Again, he glanced around and then seemed to come to a decision. 'Drink up. Let's take a walk,' indicating that it would be better to have some privacy.

They exited the pub into the evening stifling heat. Steve began to speak. 'I believe if you want answers, you should speak to the couple that came here with them.'

Des and Maria froze. 'They were with another couple?' Des gasped.

'I assumed you knew, as they came from the same country. From what they told me, this couple was the reason they came here first.'

Maria spoke first. 'Who were they, and can we speak to them?'

He shrugged. 'I suppose so, but they left here long ago and moved to Melbourne. If I remember correctly, their names were Filipe and Rosa Herrero.'

Des groaned. 'Again, it will be like looking for a needle in a haystack after all these years.'

Steve laughed. 'Not in this case. They are a household name here in Australia. They own one of the biggest transport companies. It covers most of the road, rail, shipping, and air.' He pointed at a string of nearby trucks with numerous trailers, "road trains" he called them. On the sides of these road trains were emblazoned the name "Herrero Transport." 'Just follow the name,' he added.

Just then, Des's phone rang.

# 17

Des answered the phone. 'Chaz, is that you?' he yelled.

Chaz had woken with a head that felt like it was about to explode. Not only from the copious amount of drink from the night before, but from the fact that he had uncovered so much information about his mystery family.

'No need to yell,' he replied, rubbing his temple.

Not to be deterred, Des continues to chatter excitedly. 'We have great news. There is a lead which gives us a small chance of finding out what happened to Maria's family.'

He went on to explain about the strange guy that had put them on to a couple that they had travelled together with, and that they possibly lived in Melbourne.

Chaz was surprised, as he had no expectations of them doing any better than the police. 'Great news. So you are heading here? I have some news myself,' as he explained where his investigation had led him.

'So, when are you catching up with this high diver again?' Des asked.

'Tonight. He will have more information with some luck.'

Then Des came up with a suggestion. 'If this girl is in the police, perhaps our newfound friend in the Adelaide police can help.'

Chaz laughed. 'For once, I believe you are right. If Dad could hear us talking about getting help from the police, he would disown us ! Let me know when you are heading this way. You can stay at the place I have rented. There is plenty of room.'

Des agreed and told him they would be on the first flight to Melbourne as soon as they got back to Adelaide.

Hanging up, Chaz headed for the shower to see if that would improve his headache. Twenty minutes later, he felt like a new man and decided the approach that they had taken in Adelaide could work again here. So, he looked up the headquarters of the police here in Melbourne, which he discovered was housed in The World Trade Centre in VC Docklands. Hopping in a cab, he found himself in front of an even more impressive building than they had encountered in Adelaide.

'Must in be lots of money in the police business over here,' he muttered as he made his way inside.

He entered a spacious reception area, attended by uniformed officers, looking more like receptionists at a top hotel than a cop shop. He made his way over to a young female officer. Putting on his best smile, he explained his quest to her. When he finished his story, she explained that all public records were on file and available to the general public.

'It will not have any personal details for security reasons,' she explained while directing him to a bank of computers that lined the wall.

He quickly discovered the story of James McCormack's assassination in the newspaper archive. The report said that it was believed he was undercover investigating possible terrorist groups from eastern Europe. These groups were said to have connections to Chinese splinter groups. His body was discovered in a burnt-out car. No arrests had been made. The only other thing of interest was that the article said a wife and daughter survived him.

Chaz figured it was time for some lunch and to consider his next move. He found a cafe nearby, and over a pint and a surprisingly delicious meat pie he decided to wait until that evening to see what information his friend Gavin had uncovered.

# 18

The sun was beginning to set as he made his way into The Dogs Bar to be greeted by Gavin waving to him from his usual seat. Sitting down, he gave him a hefty slap on the back. 'Glad you came back. This is the most company I have had in ages. What will you have?'

Chaz shuddered. 'Just a pint. I could not survive another night like the last.'

Gavin laughed as he ordered the drinks. 'You are letting your country down. I thought you Irish were good drinkers.'

Chaz replied with a grin. 'You must be referring to my brother.'

Gavin gasped. 'There are more of you?' Chaz filled him on the family tree. 'So, there are three McCormack's?'

'No,' corrected Chaz, 'we are the Savages.'

They chatted as Chaz filled him on his trip to police headquarters, bringing Gavin up to speed. 'I found out much the same thing,' Gavin said. 'I discovered he was deep undercover with those Serbs and Croats, but he was betrayed. The word was that it came from an informant in the police department that tipped them off. Nobody was ever charged, but on a better note, I have news on his daughter. Like her dad, she joined the police. She joined the joining terrorist squad.' He paused to take a drink, then continued. 'This is where it gets sketchy. My contacts tell me she has dropped out of sight, and any inquiries get met with stony silence.'

Chaz wondered what type of contacts this guy had to be able to get this type of information. 'Do you have her name?' he asked.

'That I can help you with. Her name is Aurora McCormack. According to records, she is 29 years' old and not married.'

Chaz nodded. 'Anything on the mother?'

Gavin pulled out a piece of paper. 'After her husband's death, she moved back to New Zealand. Here are her details,' handing him the note.

'Any address for the daughter?'

'This is where it gets extraordinary. She seems to have dropped completely out of sight; if I were a guessing man, I would wager the is gone undercover.'

Chaz began to realise where this guy was going. Is it possible that she was trying to solve her father's death? He paused to collect his thoughts. This story had taken a bizarre turn, from being a search for an old relative, now he found himself faced with the prospect of having found information pointing to somebody, only to discover that she could be in great danger.

'I have to figure out how to contact her,' looking at the note Gav had handed him. 'There is a number for her mother here. I will try to call her. I don't know how she will react to hearing from a stranger.'

Gavin butted in. 'Perhaps I can help in that regard. When she and James first met, I caught up with them by accident. I am not sure if she will remember me, but it is worth a try.'

Chaz agreed as he dialled the number. 'It's ringing,' and handed the phone to Gavin.

It seemed to ring for eternity. Finally, somebody answered. 'Hello. Is this the number for Eva McCormack?' he asked.

To Chaz's surprise, somebody asked Gavin to hold on. After a few moments, Chaz could hear someone asking who this was. Gavin went on to explain, and from the response, he guessed they remembered him. After he explained the reason for the call and their efforts in locating members of the family, describing how Chaz had traced him and, between them and the subsequent investigation, up to the dead end they had hit in his search.

She was only too happy, as she had also lost contact with her daughter. She had dropped out of sight six months ago, and her phone had been switched off. She was worried because this was not like her daughter, and to disappear without letting her know was most unusual. Chaz then spoke with her, and she pleaded with him to let her know if he had any success, then gave him all contact details she knew, which were only her telephone number and last address. She said that when she contacted her work, they said she was on compassionate leave due to the effect her father's death had on her.

Chaz promised her that if he had any success, he would be in contact, thanking her and assuring her he would do his best, not sure if his best would be of any help.

Hanging up, he and Gavin exchanged glances, 'Don't know about you, but all that seems a little strange.'

Gavin nodded. 'I seem to be at a dead end. The only people with the resources and information to mount a search were the police, and without a reasonable excuse, there was no way they could enlist their help. I guess you are out of luck unless you can get some inside help. I will keep the feelers out, but I don't hold much hope.'

A gleam came into Chaz's eye. 'Perhaps I already know somebody that could help.'

A quizzed look came across Gavin's eye. 'Who?'

Chaz grinned.

\* \* \*

Chief Inspector David George was packing up for the evening when his phone rang. Checking the number, he did not recognise it, but as this was his private number, he answered. 'Hello, who is this?'

The excited voice of Chaz greeted him. 'Hi, not sure if you will remember me, this is Chaz Savage, but we caught up in Adelaide when we were enquiring about our lost relations.'

'Chaz,' he roared. 'That didn't take long. I had a feeling I would hear from you. How is Coober Pedy?' he asked.

'Not sure,' as Chaz went on to explain how his brother and Maria followed up in Coober Pedy while he went on his quest here to Melbourne.

'Wow, you guys sure get around, so how can I help?' he asked.

Chaz told him about his search, his distant cousin's discovery, and her mysterious disappearance. There was silence on the phone for what seemed an eternity. Finally, he responded. His tone had changed. 'Give me her name. I remember something about her father's death.'

Chaz quickly gave him all he had discovered, including all the information her mother had provided.

'Leave it with me. I do not promise anything, but I will see what I can do. I will call you if I have any news. In the meantime, I would advise you not to ask too many questions. You could create trouble for her.'

Chaz thanked him and said he would wait for his call. Hanging up, he turned to his pal. 'Well, it looks like we are on hold until I hear something from this guy.'

Gavin nodded. 'Might as well have a drink. Wonder how your brother is doing?' he pondered.

## 19

## COOBER PEDY

Des had just finished booking their return to Adelaide to begin their search for this newfound connection in the search for Monica and Diego. Steve had given them some information about them, but he seemed very guarded. He supposed he did not want to be mixed up in an old murder mystery. In any case, there was not much more they could do here.

It was Maria that suggested if it was possible to see the old claim they were working on just before their disappearance. Steve agreed to take them. 'It has been deserted since they left, mainly because they had little success there, and nobody had bothered to mine it since.'

Maria was not to be deterred, wanting to at least visit where her aunt and uncle had tried to make their fortune before vanishing again. With their flight leaving for Adelaide that evening, the decision was made for Steve to drive them out for a quick look. He explained that nobody had been near for some time as that area had been picked clean.

They arrived at what, to all appearances, was just a large shallow hole in the ground, with bits of old tools scattered around. Parking, they got out to have a look around.

Des climbed down, or rather slithered, into the crater. Steve and Maria followed, and as Des started to poke around, he quickly discovered a large hole that seemed to disappear into the depths.

'Look, this is interesting!' he called out as they crowded around.

'This happened quite a lot around here. He must have broken through into an old mine,' Steve informed them.

'Well, looks as if he checked it out,' replied Des, pointing to a ladder that led down into the darkness.

'Be careful. Those old mineshafts are treacherous. I doubt they would have been mining down there,' Steve cautioned.

Not to be deterred, Des inched closer to the edge, gingerly putting a foot on the top rung of the ladder. But as soon as he put weight on it, the whole thing disintegrated and disappeared into the darkness. Des avoided following it down, falling back from the rim in a heap.

'Okay, I think we have seen enough. We better hurry if you are to make your flight,' Steve urged as if nothing had happened.

As Maria helped Des to his feet and dusted himself off, something caught his eye in the dirt where it had been disturbed after his near miss. Reaching down, he picked up the object in his hand. They all stood in shock at what he held.

It was a woman's shoe!

# 20

Chaz's flight from Melbourne landed, and he made his way out of the terminal to be greeted by his brother and Maria. It was two days since they had returned from Coober Pedy, and when they spoke to Chaz about their news, at the same time, he had just received a call from the chief inspector to tell him he had some information. But it was too sensitive to speak about over the phone, so he had agreed to fly back to catch up with him. Des had decided to wait so they could discuss all that had happened since they parted.

The chief inspector had arranged to meet at the same pub where they had lunch, which seemed a lifetime ago. The set time was for 6 pm that evening, and they had just arrived to hear the booming voice of David George calling out to them from his perch at the bar.

'All of you? I thought I was just meeting you?' as he grasped Chaz's hand in his iron grip.

'Sorry, I did not have the time to let you know. Is that a problem?' he asked.

He said, 'Too many ears around here. Get your drinks and follow me. They let me use a private room when I need a bit of privacy.'

As they collected their drinks, the chief inspector led them to what looked like a private dining room. 'Before we start, this conversation never took place, okay?' They nodded in agreement, not having a clue what was to come. 'Chaz, I don't know how but you seemed to have stumbled into a major crime investigation. When I made private inquiries about your missing relation, it stirred up a hornet's nest! It is only because I was part of the anti-terrorist force and had some good friends there that I was not shut down. As it turns out, a former partner of mine is, or I should say was, the partner of James McCormack. Since his assassination, everybody has been looking over their backs in fear of the possibility of a mole inside the force. He would not divulge much, only to say it had the highest priority.'

Chaz could not help himself. 'Had he any news about his daughter?'

'That's where it gets interesting. Of course, she was prohibited from being involved in the search for her father's killer, but he was close to her due to her father being his partner. So, he confided to me that she had taken compassionate leave so she could pursue the case. He believes she has gone underground in her search and is worried, as she had dropped out of sight.'

They gasped. 'What can we do?' Des asked.

'Nothing, you can't even say you know anything. He is working behind the scenes to see what he can do.' There was silence, then he continued. 'Even if you were to overhear me speaking about a dubious nightclub called "The Odessa Club" you would not be advised to check if that was where Aurora was hanging out.'

Chaz quickly picked up on the cue. 'Sure, there would be no point. I don't even know what she looks like.'

With that, he heard his phone ping with an incoming message. Opening the text, he found a photo of an attractive young girl. It was apparent she had inherited her mother's looks. She had shiny black hair and the powerful features of a pacific islander. She had certainly done well in the looks department, with all attributes of a film star and a top athlete. He showed the picture to his brother and Maria.

The chief inspector finished his drink, stood, and said, 'Good luck, be careful, and keep me posted. Here is the name of my old partner. You can trust him.' He strode out, handing Chaz a piece of paper without another word.

They sat silently for a moment, and then Des and Maria started talking simultaneously. 'What are you going to do?' they asked.

Chaz thought for a moment, then replied. 'What we do best. Stir things up and see what falls out!'

# 21

That evening they decided they would head back to Melbourne to continue their search. Des had located the headquarters of Herrero Transport in Melbourne. He had called them, but when he asked to speak to the owners, he was given the polite brush-off and informed that they would need an appointment. He again got a quick and definite refusal when he asked for one. They decided it would be best to pursue the matter from Melbourne.

They landed the next day and took a cab to Chaz's penthouse. 'Shit, you have gone all out with this place,' Des cried as he inspected the place.

'Try not to wreck it. I want to get my deposit back,' Chaz warned him.

Maria chipped in. 'Let's go and have something to eat. I am starving. Then we can plan our next move.'

Des groaned. 'Maria, remember this is still a very long shot. These people might not even want to talk to us. We have no idea under what circumstance they parted.'

Not to be deterred, she pointed at Chaz. 'Look what your brother has achieved. He even has the police to help. All you do is complain. Remember back in Mallorca when you did not want to search? Look what happened. You struck it rich.'

Chaz decided to put the screws on his brother. 'She is correct. You are getting too cautious.'

That got him going. 'I am not giving up. I don't want her to be disappointed.'

That was all she needed. 'Right then, it is settled. We are continuing the search. Now let's eat.'

Chaz jumped in. 'And I know just the place, and there is someone I would like you to meet.'

A puzzled look crossed their faces. 'Who?' Des asked.

He grinned. 'Just the greatest high diver that ever lived,' as he headed outside.

Gavin jumped up with delight as they entered The Dogs Bar. 'This must be the crazy brother you have been telling me about, and who is this delightful creature?' he enquired, giving a graceful bow to Maria. She blushed with delight, giving him the traditional Spanish greeting of a peck on both cheeks.

Chaz did the introductions. Then suggested moving to a table as they wanted to eat. 'That won't be a problem,' Gavin responded as he waved to the waiter. 'Our friends would like to eat. Can you fix us up with a quiet table if you can?'

The waiter escorted them to a corner nook. They ordered liver and onions, a house specialty, then Chaz began to speak. 'Gavin, I will fill you in on what I have found out about Aurora from my contact. But it would help if you did not breathe a word to anybody. It could bring trouble for him,' as he explained what he had discovered. Then he turned to Des, who told him what they had found on their visit to the old claim and the shoe's discovery. 'It could be nothing, but the reaction from the guy helping us was very strange. Seemed very anxious to get them to leave, suggesting not to mention their discovery until they had spoken to The Herrero's.'

The food arrived, and they waited until they were alone again. Gavin spoke first. 'So, to recap. Chaz, you intend to search for Aurora in the Odessa Club, home of the Yugoslav clan. Reputedly where the godfather hangs out. And you guys will try and interrogate one of the town's richest and most reclusive families.'

They nodded.

'Well, you are the Savages! I hope you don't have to live up to your name!'

# 22

**MELBOURNE**

'You have to be fucking joking,' Yakov Milosevic raged. 'Who's asking all these questions after all this time?' he roared. In front of him was Vladimir 'Vlad' Stalin. Yakov's right-hand man in the Yugoslav Clan that had formed out of the Melbourne Serbian crew, which had started in the seventies.

'Our snitch in the police thinks the daughter of the undercover cop might be involved, and, since the hit on him, she vanished. The word is that she is trying to find whoever killed her father.'

Yakov threw his hands in the air. 'One girl, how is that possible? We have word from that shit hole Coober Pedy that people have been asking questions. At the same time, this snitch tells us that somebody inside has been asking about that undercover cop and his family. This does not look like the work of a one-woman.'

Vlad offered an opinion. 'Maybe it is just coincidence. Tourists are always chasing the old history of that underground place.'

Yakov waved him off. 'I don't believe in coincidences, especially when we are so close to finally completing this deal. No, this is all the fault of that crazy bitch those nutcases insisted we use to take care of that cop.'

'Be discreet. That is all I asked. Instead, what does she do? Slices his throat like a fucking amateur,' Vlad blurted out, instantly regretting it. He got a deadly stare.

'I don't care what it is called, but thanks to her dramatic artistic exhibition, we had to burn the body. Which only helped to get the attention of the press and the politicians. Those crazy's that insisted on her, "It sends a clear message".'

Suppose they had not engaged him to deliver their requirements and the staggering amounts they had at their disposal. He would have dropped them at that point, but no matter how much money or equipment he asked for, it was immediately provided. Still, he had thought about walking away as soon as they gruesomely offed that cop. It was not because he was squeamish. He believed that whatever these guys were up to, it was better to distance themselves as much as possible, hence his reason for agreeing to clean up their mess.

But that did not explain who was making these inquiries. They had made the connection between an old unsolved murder in a mining town and the murder of an undercover policeman.

'Have they located the daughter yet?' he asked.

Vlad replied, 'The problem has been that we did not have a photo of her, but our contact inside has assured him we will have one by the end of the day.'

Yakov nodded. 'Good, as soon as you have her located, make her gone, and this time make sure it looks like a mugging or something, understand!,

He dismissed his lieutenant with a wave, returning to his thoughts. *Who are these people who seem to have discovered the connection between these events, separated by many years? Who the hell are they?*

# 23

## THE PENTHOUSE

Chaz, Des and Maria were seated on the balcony with a drink in hand. Des filled them on his conversation with their brother back home. 'He is amazed that we are still here. He could not believe you had such luck searching for our granduncle. He asked to keep them in the picture. He was catching up with Maria's dad, Bill, and agreed to bring him up to speed. He said if we needed any help to let them know.'

Maria was excited and wanted to continue with the search. 'So, what's our next move?'

Des spoke first. 'Well, if we speak to this pair, we will have to improvise. I think we will stake out the office unless you have a better idea?' The others shrugged. 'What about you, Chaz?' he asked.

'Well, I have looked up The Odessa Club, and to my surprise, it says it is located in an upmarket part of town, Turlock Gardens. Not far from The Crown Casino. It is a private club, so I thought I would catch up with Gavin to see if he can help out in that regard.'

It was then agreed they would each follow their plans and meet back later the next night. With that, Des and Maria decided on an early night.

Chaz, on the other hand, had other plans. He walked into The Dogs Bar twenty minutes later to see his friend seated in his usual spot. After he had a drink, he explained his dilemma to Gavin.

He pondered for a few minutes, then snapped his fingers. 'Sergei, he is the man we want. If anybody can get you in there, it is him. He knows everyone from that part of the world that hangs around Melbourne. He used to be the bouncer at one of the Russian clubs. I will contact him. Can you be back here tomorrow, a little earlier?' he asked.

'No problem. Do you need any cash to encourage this guy?'

Gavin laughed. 'If there is a free drink, he will be involved, don't worry.

Chaz agreed. Finishing his drink, he said. 'I will check out this place to see what clientele there is. You never know. I might even spot her.'

Gavin laughed. 'Good luck, but be careful. The guys that frequent that place may look harmless enough. But looks can be deceiving!'

Chaz stepped out of the cab at the end of the street The Odessa Club was on. 'Just drop me here. I am meeting a friend,' he told the cab driver, who looked as if he could not care if he told him he had a heart attack. Without a word, he drove away,

He discovered that a walk-by was not going to achieve much. The Odessa Club had a long-curved driveway with a valet service for the guests. From what he could see from the road, there was a steady stream of luxury cars, limos, and cabs disgorging scantily clad women hanging on to what looked like walking money. He did not want to be seen loitering around, so he beat a hasty retreat and decided to call it a night.

The following morning, Maria had Des up bright and early, excited to continue their search. 'Come on, we should be there when the place is opening. We might catch a glimpse of somebody.'

Not wanting to dampen her enthusiasm by pointing out they had no idea what these people looked like, or for that matter, whether they would have any idea what had happened to Monica and Diego. But she was not to be deterred. After a hurried breakfast, they headed out. They caught a cab to the head office of Herrero Transport, near Faulkner Street, only a ten-minute ride from their place.

Des paid for the cab at the entrance to the imposing building. 'What do we do now?' Maria asked.

He shrugged. Let's try face-to-face. You ask. They might be more receptive to a girl,' he suggested.

'Should I mention what it is about?' she asked.

He thought for a moment. 'Better keep it vague. Remember, Steve was very guarded about the whole thing. They might want nothing to do with that part of their life.'

Inside, they were greeted by a crowd of employees milling around in conversation. Wondering what was going on, Des urged Maria to do what they had agreed. 'I will hang around here and see what this is all about,' indicating the milling crowd.

Fifteen minutes later, she was back with a disappointed look crossed face. 'No luck. They were adamant that an appointment was the only way to see the owners. They suggested they could ask for one, but from their expressions, there was not much hope of that.'

Des took her hand and, with a big grin, replied. 'Come on, let's get out of here. I have everything under control.'

They hurried outside, where a confused Maria pulled him to a stop. 'What are you talking about?'

He gave her a big smile. 'Trust me. I will explain. Come on. I spotted a coffee shop just down the road. Let's get away from here, and I will explain everything.'

When they were sitting with coffee in hand, Des explained, 'All that commotion was about the plans for their annual get-together. I talked with a few of them, and they must have thought I worked there. Tomorrow, Saturday, the firm has its annual get-together. It is in a local theme park, which they own, and most importantly, there was excitement because the proprietors are supposed to be in attendance, apparently a rare occurrence.'

Maria practically jumped out of her seat. 'Fantastic, but how will we get in?'

He said nothing, just jangling an embossed card in his hand. 'No problem. I borrowed this from one of them. From what I heard them say, this is all we will need.'

She clasped the employee card in her hand. 'You are a genius.' Giving him a big hug, she asked. 'Where is this place?'

'Not far,' he replied. It is called Luna Park.'

# 24

When they returned, Chaz was about to leave for his meeting with Gavin and his Russian pal. Des quickly filled him with what they had achieved.

'I won't ask how you got that employee's card. Has it got a picture?' Chaz asked.

Des grinned. 'Do you think I came down in the last shower?' and pushed the card in his face. The picture that smiled back at him did have a passing resemblance to Des.

'Well, this thing keeps getting weirder and weirder. Now we are both connected with Luna Park,' he commented as he headed for the door.

Des hooted, 'WOO HOO, creepy.'

Chaz arrived at The Dogs Bar just before the appointed time to be greeted by the sight of a monstrous guy standing beside his mate. Chaz was 6'3" but this guy towered over him. He looked a little like Dolf Lundgren from the 'Rocky' movies, only a lot more dangerous looking!

'Meet my friend, Sergei,' Gavin said.

They shook hands, and much to his surprise, it was pretty gentle. After they got acquainted, Gavin explained that he had told his giant pal what they wanted. He gave a deep-throated laugh. 'Now that I see you, you could pass for a Russian with those looks, especially your love scratch,' referring to the scar which ran down his eyebrow, a relic from a past adventure.

After they had a few drinks and swapped tales, Chaz realised there was a lot to Gavin's past he did not know! He was thankful to have him on his side.

It was agreed that they would wait until later before heading to the club, where Sergei was sure he would know some of the guys on the door and could get Chaz in. 'Remember, once you are inside, you are on your own. It may look like a normal club but be warned. These are not nice people, so don't go asking any questions. I will tell the guys that you are a cousin of mine and are looking for your sister, who has gone off the rails, and you are trying to locate her. That is something they will believe. But nothing can happen inside. The rules are that no illegal activities of any kind are permitted. Do you understand?' he asked as he downed a triple vodka.

Chaz nodded. He assured him that things were the same back in Dublin. The only way you could enter a place like this was with an introduction. And even then, at your risk.

Two hours later, they were well-oiled, and Chaz wondered if they had forgotten about the club that night, but at midnight, Sergei indicated that they should finish up. 'Things should be getting started by now,' he announced, downing his umpteenth triple vodkas, which did not seem to affect him at all.

Outside they piled into Sergei's car, a late-model Range Rover with tinted windows. They roared off, and the fact that Sergei had consumed the best part of two bottles of vodka did not seem to concern him. 'The police don't ever bother Sergei,' he boasted.

Half an hour later, they turned into the broad driveway of the club. The line moved quickly. When they stopped, a valet attendant approached to park the car. 'No, I am not staying. I will pull to the side and won't be long,' he informed the valet.

Gavin remained in the car while Chaz and Sergei headed to the door.

'You are not coming in with me?' he asked.

The guy stopped him and then spoke. 'I am happy to help you because my friend Gavin has vouched for you. But getting killed is not in the deal. I am not sure what you are digging into, but don't include me, understand!'

Chaz nodded. It is precisely how he would have acted if the positions were reversed. 'Got you. If ever I can return the favour, I am in your debt.'

They touched knuckles as Sergei approached one of the door attendants and spoke to him in his native language. Finally, he signalled for Chaz to come. 'This is Ivan. He will look after you and give you a temporary membership card. Remember, no trouble, and good luck. You will need it,' he warned.

He turned and left Chaz to his fate.

# 25

Ivan escorted him inside. 'Keep your head down. If you spot your sister, don't get into any confrontation. Wait till you get outside, okay?'

Chaz quickly remembered Gavin's excuse for being here. 'No problem,' he assured the guy.

He sized Chaz up. 'I am on a break in a couple of hours, have a look around. Upstairs is off limits. Only the management and selected guests go up there,' he informed him as he went back to his post on the door.

Chaz headed for the bar, a colossal semi-circle that commandeered the centre of the vast main room. The walls were abutted by tables and booths, all in the style he imagined would have been in vogue in the time of the great czars of Russia.

The lighting was mellow. The lampshades were elaborate, creating deep and intimate settings, yet he felt it was almost sinister. He found a place at the bar where he had a good view of the main room and the stairs leading to the upper floor.

The place was packed with wealthy-looking guys, most accompanied by equally beautiful women. He spent the next hour nursing soda water, which still cost him small fortune. He had enough alcohol from earlier with his pals and wanted to keep his wits about him.

He saw that many beautiful young girls seemed to be from all nationalities. The only thing they had in common was that they were all staggeringly spectacular. They appeared to act as hostesses judging from their easy manner and how they interacted with the guests.

After an hour, Ivan returned. 'Any luck?' he asked as the barman placed a drink before him as if by magic.

'No, no sign. Tell me, what is the story about these girls?' nodding in the direction of one of the beauties.

Ivan smiled. 'Nice, aren't they? Most of them are students or out-of-work actresses making a little extra cash. They entertain the clientele.'

Chaz lifted his eyebrow. 'Entertain?' he asked.

Ivan was quick to respond. 'In no way. They are extremely strict in this place. The proprietors do not allow any illegal activity to occur on the premises. Whatever transpires outside is up to the individual. If your sister is into that, she is in the wrong place.'

There was a tone of suspicion in his voice. 'No, she is a little wild but a good girl. She knows what would happen to her if she stepped out of line,' Chaz assured him.

Ivan relaxed. 'Let me know if you spot her,' he added as he headed back to work.

Then there she was!

# 26

Yakov Milosevic answered his phone on the first ring. 'Well?'

'We have the photo,' came the reply. 'We are circulating it to all the places she would be likely checking out.'

Yakov stopped him. 'Make sure that they know it has to be an accident or a mugging. We can't afford any more scrutiny, not this close to the finish line.'

The voice on the other end of the phone replied, 'Understood.'

Yakov sat back in his chair. He could not shake this uneasy feeling. He hoped it was because he had to interact with that crazy Chen Wah Yim. He was the leader of this splinter group called "Tsunami", which he knew translated to "Silent wave".

'That is what we will be to the corrupt government of this country and the foreigners that inhabit it,' Chen had told Yakov on their first meeting.

Now, as then, Yakov put it down to the rantings of another of militant group that sprang up around the world from time to time. He would probably have put a bullet in his head just to shut him up if not for the staggering amount of chash they had offered. What they required from him was access to his smuggling network to deliver a particular piece of equipment. What they were, he had no idea and did not care so long as they paid. Thanks to the unique position he had found himself in a year ago, he could provide that service.

*Now it was down to the final phase, and he could wipe his hands of these nutcases.*

# 27

## THE ODESSA CLUB

Chaz reacted as soon as he saw her. He had no doubt he had found his long-lost relation. She bore minimal resemblance to the photo his police mate had provided.

She was stunning, at least six feet tall, and had all the curves to match. Her hair was shining black, set-in dread knots intertwined with brilliant colour treads—like a Jamaican dancer.

He saw she was working as a hostess, so he acted. As soon as he saw her move in his direction, he stood and bumped into her as if by accident. 'So sorry,' he cried.

Her reaction was odd. Barely making eye contact, she shrugged. 'It is not a problem,' as she went to move on.

'At least let me buy a drink to make up for my clumsiness,' he said, slightly louder than necessary.

She glanced around, obviously not wanting to draw attention. She realised that refusing would be strange, seeing as that was what she was meant to do. Get the punters to spend. 'That would be lovely,' she replied, sitting beside him. She ordered a champagne cocktail, which he got no change from a A$100 note.

'Let's take a table, it will be more comfortable,' he suggested.

She nodded absently, her attention elsewhere. When they were seated, he could observe her more closely. She was wearing a simple little black dress, which was anything but simple. She wore little makeup, just some eyeliner and a slash of red lipstick to accent her glamorous lips.

'What should I call you?' he asked.

'You can call me Candy,' she replied.

'Family liked sweet things?' he quipped.

It fell on deaf ears as her eyes darted around. If this was her attempt at undercover, he was amazed she had survived this long. 'Do you come here often?' he asked, with a grin on his face.

'Really? That's your chat up line?' she responded.

'Well, it worked, didn't it? At last, I got a reaction,' he chuckled.

A flush filled her face. 'Sorry, I am not myself this evening,' she replied.

'You can say that again,' he mumbled under his breath.

'What did you say?' she asked.

Chaz smiled, replying. 'I was saying that I agree with you. We all have days like that.' She began to relax. He continued. 'I know it is hard to understand my accent. We Irish talk too fast.'

'Not at all. I love the Irish Accent. It reminds me…' She stopped, realising she was saying too much.

'Of what?' he asked.

Flustered, she quickly said, 'All the great film actors that come out of there.'

He decided to let her off the hook. 'You sound like you come from here, but your looks, that's another thing.'

For the first time, she smiled. 'My mother is Polynesian. I guess that's why I look different,' she answered.

*And beautiful*, he thought. 'Was she the one that named you Candy?

That broke the ice a little. 'None of the girls that work here use their real name. It saves being bothered,' she explained.

He laughed. 'I agree. That's why I go under the name of Chaz!'

She laughed back. 'Okay, very funny. Maybe another time we can share names.'

While this conversation was going on, Chaz noticed three guys that seemed to be glancing in their direction. Usually, he would have put it down to them checking Aurora out. But considering the circumstances, he decided to keep an eye on them. After a short while, the guys finished their drinks and left, and he relaxed as he considered his next move.

'Thank you for the drink and the refreshing conversation. I have to be going now,' she said as she stood to leave.

Chaz jumped up. 'I hope that we can meet again,' he said, clasping her hand.

She gently extracted it. 'You never know, do you come here often?' she snickered.

'I will, from now on,' he replied.

'Well then…' She left the sentence unfinished.

'Do you need a lift home?' he asked.

'I am good. My car is parked out back. That way, I can avoid all that nonsense outside.'

She waved goodbye as she glided towards the door.

## 28

Chaz waited a couple of minutes, then followed. After being lucky enough to have located his distant relative, he would not lose sight of her now.

Ivan was still at the door. 'Any luck?' he asked as Chaz passed him by. 'On her trail as we speak,' as he headed in the direction of the carpark.

As he rounded the corner, he spotted Aurora making for a line of cars. At that exact moment, from the corner of his eye, he saw merging from the shadows the three characters he had seen inside. They headed directly for her with obvious bad intentions.

'Aurora!' he roared at the top of his voice as he charged toward them.

They reacted in shock at the sound of his cry. At the same time, a shocked Aurora responded to the sound of her name. The biggest of the guys turned to confront Chaz.

'Fuck off if you don't want to get hurt!' he snarled.

Chaz delivered a powerful kick to his privates, dropping him to his knees. Without missing a stride, Chaz gave a knee directly under the stricken guy's chin, which would put him in hospital for a long time.

With one out of the fight, he carried on without stopping to inspect his handy work. Chaz was in his element. This was not a movie, and fights did not go on for half an hour. It was usually quick and brutal, and he was good at it. No talking, get the job done. Not like the fool that just tried to tell him not to get hurt.

Next in line, the guy who just made the mistake of stepping in front of his pal, taking him out of play.

Second mistake: reaching into his jacket for some weapons. As he reached with his right hand inside his jacket, Chaz hit him with a right cross directly on the chin line. The blow would have stunned a horse.

Second one down.

Chaz leaped onto the stricken guy, now collapsed. His legs had crossed as he fell, and as Chaz's big frame landed on them, the sound of breaking bones was music to his ears.

He was fully expecting an attack from the final guy. To his surprise, he was greeted by the sight of him lying on the ground in a pool of blood. Aurora was standing over him with an extendable baton in her hand.

She held it threateningly at Chaz. 'Who the hell are you, and how do you know my name?' she demanded.

He held up his hands in surrender. 'All good questions, but don't you think it would be better if we did it elsewhere?' he pleaded. Then he began to search the attackers for clues. As he was rifling through their pockets, she continued. 'They must have followed you. Who are you?

He did not reply. He just held up a photo of her that he had taken from the pocket of one of them. 'Did I give them these also?'

Still in shock from hearing this stranger calling her name, she continued to try to make sense of it. 'They must have been muggers,' she said without much conviction.

He held up stuffed wallets and then showed her the Rolex watch one was wearing. 'They were targeting you. I thought you were a cop. This was a hit!' he said, holding up a Glock he had taken out of the guy's pocket. 'Where is your car?'

She pointed to a silver-grey Land Cruiser parked at the far end of the row.

'Time for us to leave. I am sure. As a cop, you won't want to answer any questions about this.'

She did not need any prompting. They bolted to the car, and as they ran, she opened the doors using the remote. As they jumped in, she turned to Chaz. 'What are you doing?'

He could not believe his ears. 'Same as you, getting the hell out of here. Remember, I am the guy that just came to your aid.'

'Thanks, but who are you?' she persisted.

Chaz roared, 'We can sit here, and when the cops come, you can hear the whole story back at the station, or we can go somewhere, and I will be glad to sit and chat with you over a drink!'

That seemed to satisfy her. She gunned the car out onto the driveway and took off at breakneck speed.

Chaz gripped the armrest. 'If I could suggest, perhaps, slow down to something approaching the speed limit. The last thing we need is to be pulled over for speeding.'

She gradually reduced the speed without replying and spoke without turning her head. 'Okay, who are you, and how do you know my name?'

Chaz commenced to tell her the story, condensing it as much as he could. He began with his mother's request to locate her long-lost uncle, concluding with their meeting at the club. He decided not to mention his assistance from his cop mate in Adelaide, also excluding his brother's search for another long-lost relative. That would be too much. He figured his story was enough for one day.

She shook her head in disbelief, trying to make sense of what she had just heard. 'But how did you recognise me?' she asked.

Not wanting to mention the photo he had been given, he decided to fudge the truth. 'Your old friend Gavin helped put me in touch with your mother. She gave me an almost perfect description of you. You a pretty distinctive looking woman, you know,' he added.

That brought a slight upturn of her lips as she tried not to smile. 'Did she ask why you were trying to locate me?'

Chaz did not want to get into many details, so he replied, 'No, she was more concerned that you had dropped out of sight and had not returned her calls. I would suggest you give her a call. She is worried.' This put a sad expression on her face. Wanting to get her focus back on the present, Chaz changed the subject. 'Want to tell me where you are heading?' he asked.

She shook her head. 'Just driving until I can figure this out. I can't understand how they located me. Are you sure they did not follow you?'

He shook his head. 'No, I spotted them in the club. They knew whom they were looking for. Remember the photo. So, wherever you are staying, I would forget about going there.'

She looked at him. 'Well, I don't have much choice. All my stuff is there.'

He thought for a moment. 'Okay, here is what we will do. Drive to your place, and pick up what you need. You can come back to where I am staying. There is plenty of room for you until we figure out the next move.'

Again, she asked. 'What do you mean, we?'

He grinned. 'We Savages are a very tight family. Now that I have found you, I am obliged to be your knight in shining armour!'

This brought another grin as she headed off toward her abode.

# 29

It was almost dawn when they pulled up in front of a large apartment building in Essendon on the northwest outskirts of Melbourne.

Chaz checked around for any suspicious activity and then turned to Aurora. 'Looks all clear to me. I will go in with you to collect what you need.' She started to object, but he stopped her. 'Look, I don't know what's going on, and it looks as if you are not sure either, so until we figure things out, we will stick together.'

She shrugged. 'Why would you get involved in this? You don't even know me?'

Chaz grinned. 'That's what we Savages do. Better get used to it,' as he began to usher her out of the car, then stopped. 'Is there somewhere we could put the car out of sight?'

'There's a back entrance for deliveries. We could park there for a bit,' she said. 'You seem to have some experience in this sort of thing.'

'Just a concerned citizen doing his civic duty,' he said, as they pulled around the corner.

Aurora quickly collected things she might need for a few days. At the same time, Chaz kept an eye out of the window, where he had an unobstructed view of the street and the entrance. His suspicions were quickly confirmed. Just as Aurora said she was ready, a black 7-series BMW pulled up outside, and four tough-looking dudes exited.

'Shit, you sure seemed to have stirred up a hornet's nest. These guys are persistent,' he said, indicating what was happening outside. 'Is there a back entrance we can use to get to the car?'

She nodded, indicating for him to follow. A couple of minutes later, they were in the car and had driven far away before their pursuers reached the apartment. 'Who owns the apartment?' he asked.

'A friend of mine is overseas for a couple of months,' she replied.

'That's good. What about the car, is it registered to you?'

She shook her head. 'No, it is one of the many cars we seize for many reasons. We use them for undercover work. They will run up against a brick wall if anybody tries to trace them.'

A frown crossed his face. Then he replied, 'Let's wait until we are in my place, and then we can discuss our next move,' as they lapsed into silence.

Chaz found himself thinking. *What had his newfound relative got herself into? The amount of attention she was causing seemed to him overkill. As for the car, if it came from the pound, one group of people could trace it. The police!*

# 30

Des and Maria arrived at their "employees' party" at Luna Park. They had no idea what reception they would receive, or for that matter, if they did succeed in meeting with the reclusive Herrero's, what their reaction would be.

They were surprised at the size of the crowd. There had to be at least five hundred people at the entrance waiting to be allowed inside. They did not need to be concerned about their pass being inspected. As the gates opened, the crowd surged through the gaping clown mouth entrance. Des and Maria followed the crowd inside, thankful that nobody seemed concerned about checking credentials. Some staff were dressed up as famous Disney characters such as Micky Mouse, Donald Duck, Buzz Lightyear, and many others. It was clear that no expense had been spared. There were pavilions set up with different themes. Some had groups playing all styles of music, from Jazz to Rock 'n' Roll. All of the rides were open and free to everybody. For those that preferred, dining was available in several areas, with a full bar available.

As they wandered around getting their bearings, Des could not help mentioning what was on his mind. 'This must be costing a fortune. If these are the friends of your aunts, I am not sure how we will be received asking them about your aunt's disappearance and an age-old murder.'

He got no response from Maria. Her focus was firmly on locating the Herrero's. The question of how they would approach them was not on her mind.

They wandered through the amusement park, mingling with the crowd for the next hour. They were engaged in small talk with some of the staff from time to time, discreetly asking when the big bosses would appear. But all they could discover was that it was only for a fleeting visit when they occurred.

They were starting to think they were out of luck when a buzz of activity from the crowd attracted their attention. Everybody was heading for a sizeable accessible area where the attendants had set up a small platform. Then, surrounded by staff, the people that everybody had been waiting for appeared.

They were loved and respected by all in attendance, judging by their reaction. Des and Maria wormed their way forward until they could get a good look at them. They were greeted by the appearance of a couple in their early sixties. They were elegantly dressed and greeted everybody around them with friendly gestures. They occasionally stopped to exchange a word or two with people they recognised.

Des got the feeling he had seen the woman before and turned to Maria to say something when he realised she was shaking uncontrollably. 'What's wrong?' he asked, taking her in his arms.

She did not respond. Instead, she pushed free, gripping his hand as she propelled them to the front. Before Des could react, he found themselves facing the surprised couple. Maria stepped up to the lady with a shocked expression on her face.

'Hello, my name is Maria,' she announced, pausing for a moment, then continued. 'My mother is Meris Gonzales. From Mallorca.'

The lady's reaction was to freeze on the spot while gripping her husband's hand for support. People started to rush forward, but she raised her hand to stop them. She paused for a moment to compose herself. Then she began to speak.

'Welcome all. We are so happy to have you share our success again this year. None of this would have been possible without your participation. Please enjoy the day.' Then she turned to her shocked husband and whispered. 'We need some privacy.'

He reacted at once, signalling to an attendant. 'Please take us somewhere that we can have some privacy.' The staff responded at once. 'Please follow me,' indicating to them the direction. As they began to move, the lady stopped. 'Please, I would like this young lady to accompany us,' she instructed, pointing at Maria.

'I am with her,' Des yelled as he saw the attendants moving in to keep the crowd back.

'Of course, please accompany us,' indicating to allow Des through.

They made their way to what seemed to be an old house that had been converted into offices with a sitting room attached to entertain special guests. When seated, Felipe Herrero instructed the staff to give them privacy. As soon as they were alone, he turned to his wife. 'What is happening, my dear? Who are these people?' he asked.

'Look at this young lady. Now look at me.'

He did as instructed, a look of confusion on his face. Then as if hit by a bolt of lightning, he froze on the spot. 'No, it is not possible,' he gasped.

That was the moment it hit Des. He realised why he thought he knew this woman. She looked remarkably similar to Maria's mother. Before he could speak, Rosa Herrero said, 'Enough, it is time,' gripping her husband's hand.

She looked him in the eyes as their gaze met, and he gave a perceptible nod. Then she spoke.

'Maria, I am your aunt. We are Diego and Monica Suarez!'

# 31

## COOBER PEDY
## 1972

Diego burst out of the door of the bar. He was still seething with rage from Felipe's betrayal. He needed to clear his head and walked over to Steve's car yard. He was the only one that he trusted in this place. He opened the door as soon as he knocked.

'Hello, my friend, what brings you around at this time of night?' he asked as he invited him in.

'I have a huge problem,' he said as his friend placed a beer in his hand. Steve sat down as Diego explained what had happened and how Felipe had spilled the beans about their nest egg.

He had told Steve about their windfall in the past, and he had advised them not to speak of it to anyone. A worried look crossed his face.

'George Pratt is sure to try and get revenge. Especially now that he knows you have those diamonds.'

Diego nodded. 'What do you think we should do?' he asked.

Steve shook his head. 'I think you know there is only one thing to do.'

Diego nodded in agreement. 'I know we have to get out of here, and the sooner, the better. What do you suggest?'

Without hesitation, he replied. 'First thing, don't wait for the bus. You are sure to be spotted. I will locate a truck heading to Adelaide and arrange a lift. I suggest you head back and get what you need, and tomorrow I should have something organised.'

They finished their drinks, and Diego returned to inform Monica what they needed to do. As passed the bar, he could still hear what had happened being discussed inside. So decided to head back to their place. When he stepped in, he was rocked by two arms wrapped around his neck. It was Monica in floods of tears.

'You are alive. Everybody was saying that you had gone to confront George. They were saying one of you would get killed.'

He calmed her down and explained what he had been doing. She was relieved and hurriedly agreed. 'We don't need anything. I am wearing everything we need,' indicating the long skirt she was wearing. It contained the diamonds, which were sewn into the hem.

'Before we leave, we should tell Felipe and Rosa. She at least deserves to know why we are going. He reluctantly agreed and headed over to speak to them. It was only across the road, but they realised the Ute was missing when they arrived.

'Let's wait inside. I am afraid of standing here,' Monica said.

He retrieved the spare hidden key, and let themselves inside. They must have dozed off but were awakened by a loud commotion. Somebody was shouting.

'George is dead. I found him by the foreigner's claim. His head is bashed in. It looks like the Diego guy finished the job.'

Monica and Diego sat in stunned silence, unable to believe their ears. Diego leapt to his feet. 'I am going to speak to them.'

Before he could move, Monica grabbed him. 'You will do no such thing. Are you crazy? You just beat the hell out of that guy. Nobody is going to believe you did not finish the job.'

He looked at her with fear in his eyes. Then an idea dawned. 'I'll be okay,' he said, kissed her, and then went to the door.

Monica gasped as he stepped outside, thinking the worst. But within a couple of minutes he was back safe, albeit shaken and pale. He then explained his and Felipe's similar appearance. The crowd, seeing him emerging from The Herrero's place, had mistaken him for Felipe.

'What should we do now?' he gasped.

Monica thought for a moment. Then a gleam came into her eyes. 'We vanish!'

# 32

'And that night, our friend Steve spirited us away to Adelaide.'

Monica then explained how they had moved to Melbourne, bought a long-haul truck, and built that one truck into an international transport company. All while operating under the Herrero name.

Maria could not contain herself, throwing her arms around her long-lost aunt. 'I knew when I saw you. It was like I was looking at my mother,' she cried as they embraced.

Des decided to step in. 'Let me introduce myself and explain how we are standing here together.'

Felipe, or more correctly, Diego, nodded in agreement. 'A perfect suggestion, but before we start, I believe a drink is in order.'

As soon as the refreshments arrived, they had privacy. Des got everybody seated and began the tale of their journey from his arrival on Mallorca, his discovery of the Nazi treasure and the note that Diego and Monica had left, which triggered the search for Maria's long-lost relatives, finally bringing them up to their meeting today.

'I am sure you have a million questions, as do we. But I think, with your permission, we should let your sister know that we have located you. Agreed?'

Monica and Maria were in tears but at once agreed. 'Before we call, I suggest you don't get into too much detail on the phone.' He could see the confusion on their faces. 'For example, I would not get into you using different names.'

Diego glanced at his wife with concern. 'Of course. It will take some time to explain all that to them.'

For the next two hours, the long-lost sisters and all the relations had to have their turn speaking. Des and Diego sat to one side while Des related events, including what was going on with Chaz, to his brother Vincent and Maria's father, Bill.

'Enough!' Vincent Savage QC interjected. 'This is too important an event to be discussed over a telephone (he still refused to call it a mobile) 'It requires a good setting and a drink in hand, and from what I have overheard from the other conversation, most of us. And that includes Bill, who is giving the thumbs up. I expect we will be on the next available flight. Fix us up with nice accommodations,' he instructed, then hung up.

'That's my lawyer brother. Always thinks he is in front of a jury,' Des explained to Diego. Who, to this point, had not said much.

Des decided not to push him. This must be a lot for him to process. The finding of his bag with the message and, as a result, the reconnection with his wife's family. All this was going on, plus the elephant in the room. What was the story about the name switch? He could not imagine the turmoil he must be feeling.

*So much for a relaxing holiday, Chaz. You won this toss!*

# 33

Chaz opened the penthouse door, allowing an astonished Aurora to enter.

'What are you, a drug dealer?' she asked as she looked around at the opulent setting.

'That hurts. I have just saved you from who knows what? And all I get is to be accused of being a scumbag drug dealer, just like a cop. Always thinking the worst!'

She dropped her head sheepishly. 'Well, you must admit this is a lot to process, and now you present this place! What am I supposed to think?'

He shrugged. 'Come on, let's get you settled. I am only renting this place.'

He left her to get cleaned up while he headed into the kitchen. Aurora reappeared soon after, towelling her hair, she piled it on top of her head and enveloped it with the towel. 'I hope you don't mind me borrowing one of your robes?' she asked.

'Knock yourself out,' he said, as he handed her a drink. 'I have fixed something to eat, and I popped a bottle of wine. I hope a Sauvignon Blanc is okay?'

She nodded. 'Compared to the piss we have to drink in the club. Anything would be okay.' Taking the glass, she slugged a big gulp, then smacked her lips. 'Perfect,' she announced.

Chaz brought out a platter with cheese and a selection of meats and olives. He placed them on a coffee table as Aurora curled up on the couch and dived in. He sat down opposite her. 'Okay, why don't you explain why those guys were trying to hurt you?' he asked her.

She shrugged. 'I suppose it must have something with my trying to find out who killed my father.'

Chaz looked at her in confusion. 'But you are with the police. I understand that perhaps they don't want you going vigilante. But why were they not investigating his death?'

She snorted. 'That's the problem. Somehow this has become a political football. He was investigating a new Chinese splinter group called Tsunami, which had been put on the terrorist watch list. There had been chatter that something was coming down the pipeline. Dad was making some inquiries about a tip he had received from an informant when suddenly he and his partner started to get some pushback and found they were being impeded at every turn. So dad decided to do some digging on his own. He didn't even want to tell his partner.'

Chaz was perplexed. 'So, he did not trust anyone?' he asked.

'No,' she replied. 'Luckily, I was staying at his apartment when I got news of his death. So, before I left, I collected his notebooks and his laptop. Luckily I did, because before the police went there, somebody ransacked the place.' She took a sip of wine and continued, 'In his notes, he referred to a tip he was investigating about the involvement of a major Australian company, and if word got out, they were looking at them. It could cause a huge stink, so he decided to work alone to protect his partner. They were staunch friends.'

'Sounds like you have a big rat in your organisation,' he added.

She nodded. 'So, how about you tell me how a long-lost relative can afford a place like this?'

Chaz began by explaining that the adventure that his brothers and a local family had been involved in on the island of Mallorca had resulted in them being set pretty comfortably.

'So, there are three of you. What are you guys? Some modern-day Robin Hoods?' she asked.

Chaz laughed. 'Probably not. More like we seem to end up in weird situations. Look at what has happened here. I came looking for a long-lost relative. Then when I locate you, I find myself mixed up in some gang-related attempt on your life. I guess that happens when you are related to this family.'

Before Aurora could respond, the sound of the door opening brought her to her feet in shock. 'Who is that?' she whispered.

'Relax, it is just Des and Maria. They are staying here as well.'

They appeared in the living room, full of excitement. 'Great news,' Des shouted. Then he froze in shock at this strange woman standing in a dressing gown with a towel wrapped around her head.

There was silence for a moment, then Chaz interjected. 'Guys, meet your distant cousin. Aurora, this is my crazy brother, Desmond, and his girlfriend, Maria.'

'You found her!' Des gasped, rooted to the spot.

Maria rushed forward. 'I can't believe it. If it were not for these guys, I would never have believed it,' grasping Aurora's hand, then hugging her. She then broke away. 'This is amazing. We have news as well. You won't believe what has happened.'

There was silence when she realised they were waiting for her to continue. She blurted out with a wild yell, 'We have found my aunt and uncle.'

# 34

Across the city, while the Savage brothers and Aroura were having their reunion, Christine Wolfe was answering her phone.

Recognising the number, she stepped outside her office away from prying ears. Although her phone was encrypted, she still did want to be in earshot of anybody.

'Hello, my darling.'

But before she could continue, the caller cut her off in his Eaton-educated accent. The caller was the Right Honourable Cyril Stanford, Deputy Prime Minister, alongside his arch-enemy Prime Minister Michael 'Mick' Parker. Parker was a working-class man who had worked himself through the ranks to the top job. He was the darling of the people. The polar opposite of Stanford, a self-made millionaire who had made his fortune in the 80s in the whitegoods boom, much to the displeasure of his titled, highbrow family.

Selling up when the trend peaked, he retired to Australia and entered politics. A single man with all the appearances of his titled background, along with his good looks, he soon became the darling of the "It crowd".

Unfortunately, his success in politics was hindered by the very same attributes. The growing independence movement had marred his tilt at the top job.

'What news have you got on that girl? She may already know too much if she has her father's laptop. If so, it could bring this whole thing down.'

The voice on the other end replied in a whisper. 'They found her, but she got away.'

'What?' he roared. 'How could that Serb idiot have messed up getting rid of a slip of a girl?'

She rushed to calm him down. 'She had help. Whoever he was, he disposed of three of his best guys. But don't worry, we now know what car she is using. It won't be long before she slips up, my darling.'

He grunted. 'Well, I hope for both our sakes that you are right. Keep me informed.'

'Of course. Are we still catching up this evening?' she asked breathlessly.

'I will let you know. You know we have to be discreet.'

She sighed deeply. 'I miss you so much, my darling. I am taking a terrible risk as well, you know. I need to see you,' she pleaded.

'Don't worry, my love, when I am Prime Minister. You will be at my side. I promise you. Now find that bitch!' as he hung up.

She stood, staring at the phone in her hand, lost in thought when a voice snapped her back to the present. 'Police Commissioner, you are needed in the situations room,' her aide reminded her.

'Thanks, be there in a moment,' she replied.

# 35

At the penthouse, the newfound friends shared the events that brought them to this point.

Chaz had filled them in on the events leading up to his discovery of Aurora at the club and his confrontation with the guys. Which brought a sly grin to Aurora's face. 'I am very grateful to Chaz. I don't know what the outcome would have been if he had not arrived when he did.'

Embarrassed, Chaz tried to change the subject. 'Why don't you guys fill us in on how you found your aunt.'

Maria took up the story, explaining how this guy in Coober Pedy had led them to Melbourne in their search. 'Desmond came up with the brilliant idea of gate-crashing their annual work event.' Unlike his brother, Des was revelling in the compliments. Maria continued, explaining that when they saw them, she immediately recognised the similarities between her mother and the subsequent reunion.

Chaz interjected. 'Strange the coincidence that I discovered the link to locate Aurora in the same place you did.'

Des jumped in. 'Even more strange is that their company owns the park.'

'What's their company called?' Chaz asked.

'Herrero Transport,' he replied.

Aurora leapt to her feet with a gasp. 'I can't believe it. That's the company my dad was investigating for links to the Chinese terrorist group.'

Maria's face became very grim. 'Are you suggesting that my aunt and uncle are involved with some terrorist group?'

Chaz jumped in. 'Hold on, let's not jump to conclusions. None of us has enough information to figure out what's going on. Remember, we are all trying to catch up with the strange and confusing events of the last few days. I know from talking to Aurora and some inquiries I have made that something bizarre is happening.'

Aurora took over. 'Chaz is right. I am sorry, Maria. I was only shocked to hear that your relation's company was the one my father was interested in. I was not accusing them of anything.'

Des spoke next. 'I agree. We should all calm down. Our priority should be to get together with Mona... sorry, Felipe and Rosa.' Not wanting to mention the name switch in front of a police officer, he said, 'Why don't we go and see them? We arranged to go to their house as soon as we collected Chaz. Why don't we all go together, and maybe we can get to the bottom of this mystery?'

# 36

The taxi slowed as it approached the gated entrance to the mansion that dwarfed the surrounding properties in the upmarket suburb of Toorak. They looked in amazement at the splendour of the gardens as they travelled up the driveway to be greeted by the sight of a three-storey house that looked like it had been transplanted from a grand estate in England.

'Must be a heap of money moving things around this place,' Chaz commented.

The front door sprung open, and Monica and Diego greeted them. Hugs and kisses were shared as hurried introductions were made. Des quickly referred to Monica and her husband as their aunt and uncle, avoiding mentioning names. They followed the couple into the sitting room, the size of a small tennis court. Yet, despite its size, it exuded a feeling of warmth.

After they were seated, attendants provided everybody with refreshments and then retired to leave the excited group in privacy. To Chaz's surprise, Des decided to take care of the introductions, starting with Chaz. 'This is my brother, Chaz, and this is Aurora.' Before he could continue, Monica blurted out in Spanish, 'Que Guapa Esposa.' 'What a beautiful wife.'

A puzzled expression on their faces prompted Maria to speak, 'No, this is not his wife. It's his cousin.'

There was silence for a second then they all started to laugh. Des took the opportunity of the break in the conversation and turned to Monica and Diego before they could speak again.

'Before you mention your name, we should tell you that our new cousin is a member of the police. She is trying to find out who killed her father. He was a policeman also. Because of reasons she can explain to you if she chooses, she is acting on her own without the authorities behind her.' He then turned to Aurora. 'Our relatives are about to reveal information that has nothing to do with your case but could perhaps be viewed as a police matter. So, I suggest you listen as our cousin rather than a cop, agreed?'

She replied at once. 'I am here for only one thing. To find who killed my father. So speak freely, and I will do the same.'

Des visibly relaxed, nodding to the couple to speak. They told their story of how they had swapped names with their companions. As time passed, they had their first child very soon after arriving in Melbourne. They decided for the safety of Christine and her son, Miguel Herrero. After the arrival of their daughter, they had no choice but to continue.

Pausing to take a drink, Aurora asked, 'But with your position in the community and the resources at your disposal, surely any good lawyer could have that matter easily settled?'

Diego looked at Monica, who gave a perceptible nod. 'I can tell you how many times we thought about telling the children, but I am ashamed to say I was the one that decided not to in the end. Then, when Miguel graduated and got a job as a political analyst with the major party, I couldn't do it. His career has taken off. A scandal like this would ruin him.'

Maria asked. 'What about your daughter?'

Monica smiled. 'Christine is a doctor. She specialises in paediatrics'. She works in a hospital in South Africa. She would not be a problem. She is involved in many civil rights movements. She would laugh and say, go for it!' she laughed.

Diego continued. 'That was the worst problem until a year ago.' Pausing again to take a drink, it was apparent they had something grave on their mind. He glanced at Monica again. Taking a deep breath, he continued, 'That was when that Eastern European thug appeared!'

# 37

**MELBOURNE**
**1 YEAR AGO**

Felipe was on his regular morning walk when he became aware of someone alongside him. Glancing, he saw a tough-looking character dressed in a fashionable tracksuit. 'Good morning, Diego. How are you?' the guy enquired.

Hearing that name hit him like a thunderbolt. 'I am afraid you are confusing me with someone else,' he blurted out.

The guy smirked. 'I don't think so, Señor Diego Suarez. Who came from the Island of Mallorca. No, it is you, Diego, and your lovely wife, Monica, waiting patiently for your return so you can go on your weekly lunch date,' he replied.

Diego glanced around in terror.

'If I wanted to harm you or your family, I would have done it weeks ago,' the guy added. 'Now, I suggest we go back to your wonderful mansion to discuss how you can save this grand empire of yours.'

At Diego's reluctance, he urged him by displaying the Glock he had in his armpit holster. Fifteen minutes later, they were seated in the living room, with a dazed Monica gripping her husband's hand in terror.

The fellow began to speak. 'First of all, I want to assure you I wish you nor your family no harm, and with a little cooperation from you and I can guarantee that all evidence of your past adventures will disappear. And I will be out of your lives.'

Diego responded. 'So, what do you want of us, money or what?'

'My apologies. I just remembered that I had to introduce myself. My name is Yakov Milosevic. You may have heard of me. The press says I am the leader of the "Yugoslav Clan." Which I am, by the way. So why would I want your money?' He answered himself. 'What we want is the use of your transport system. And before you ask, the answer is no. We do not want you to transport drugs. We can take care of that ourselves,' he replied with an evil grin on his face. 'All we require is for you to transport some pieces of machinery over the next few months.'

Confused, Diego asked, 'But why do you need our company to bring in machinery? Any transport company could do that?'

Again, the grin. 'Because yours is the only one that can transport military equipment. And again, before you ask. It is not guns or any explosives—just complex machinery. I don't understand it myself. The people that asked for it did not tell me, and I did not ask.' He paused, then his face turned to ice. 'Before you even consider refusing. I want you to know that doing so would endanger you and your son, Miguel, in Canberra. Even your daughter, Christine, in South Africa would be at risk. So, choose carefully.'

# 38

**MELBOURNE**
**PRESENT DAY**

'So, you can see we were left with little choice,' Monica said.

Chaz spoke up. 'Time to take a break and gather our thoughts. I am sure you all have a bunch of questions. But Diego, could we have some more drinks before we continue?'

He jumped up. 'Of course,' picking up the phone and speaking to somebody in rapid Spanish.

While the food and drinks were carried and arranged on the dining table, Chaz took Des and Aurora aside. 'I think we have found the connection between your dad's assassination. Somebody did not want a connection between the Herrero's and the case your father was working on.'

Aurora nodded. 'From what I have been able to find from his laptop, he was investigating a sinister Chinese group. From what I could decipher, they are planning a major event.'

Des interjected. 'Aurora, you don't know us at all, but I will say something I will probably regret. But Chaz is the one I would put my faith in for this puzzle. He has a way of seeing things others can't.'

Aurora was silent a moment, then spoke. 'All I want is to find out who killed my father. So far, all I have done is hit dead ends, so yes, I have seen your brother in action. Count me in.'

Chaz nodded and began to speak. 'I suggest until we figure out what is going on. We have a couple of priorities. The first is to keep our connection with Monica and Diego to ourselves until we can figure out a plan. The second is to make sure that Aurora does not have to keep looking over her shoulder.'

Des nodded. 'I agree. The first should be easy. We are the only ones that know the connection. Aurora is another matter. From the looks of it, these people are determined to stop her poking her nose in their plans.'

There was a mumble of agreement from the others. Chaz stepped in. 'I have an idea that might put us in a position to dissuade them, but we need more information about this Chinese lot and what they are up to. That seems to be the connection to you guys,' pointing at the Herrero's. 'And I think, for the time being, you should continue with your arrangement until we know a little more. On that point, I have a question. How many packages have you delivered?' he asked.

Diego replied. 'To date, three. They told us the next one would be the final one.'

Des questioned, 'How does it work?'

Diego replied, 'We are informed when it will be at the docks. We then collect it and clear all customs and government requirements. Then we transport it to a destination just over the NSW border. After that, we have no idea where it goes.'

'Same drop-off point?' Chaz asked.

'No. It is a different one every time and another courier,' Diego replied.

Des continued. 'Any idea when the final one will be?'

Diego shrugged. 'No, we receive a call with instructions. But judging from the frequency and the urgency in this voice the last time he called, I imagine it will be very soon.'

Chaz retook charge. 'Okay, no time to waste. Aurora, do you trust your father's partner?' he asked.

She nodded vigorously. 'He and my dad were very close. Not only were they partners forever, but also staunch friends.'

He nodded. 'Good, we will need as many friends as possible to beat these guys. Reach out to him, but for safety, don't divulge where you are staying. Just let him know you are okay and lying low now.'

She nodded reluctantly. 'If you are thinking of using him for information. That won't work. He and my father were convinced there was a mole at the highest-level feeding information and blocking any information sources.'

Chaz smiled. 'That's exactly why we need him on our side. He will be useful if we need to spread disinformation later,' he replied.

She looked puzzled. 'Okay, but we could do with somebody on the inside to access resources.'

Again, he smiled, glancing at Des. 'Don't worry. I have someone in mind. I will call him shortly to see if he will help,' he replied.

Aurora could not help herself. 'What is it with you guys? You are only in this country a couple of weeks and already you seem to be outpacing any official investigation. Are you some secret vigilante group?'

It was Maria that answered. 'No. They are much more than that. My mother believes they are saviours sent from Heaven. But I think they are three men with extraordinary talents born out of their past. But I like the name she has given them, "The Umbrella Men".' Seeing the looks of confusion, she continued. 'When they take you under their umbrella, you feel safe.'

Chaz interjected. 'We are none of that. It is just that we seem to find ourselves in these weird situations.'

Des decided to have his say. 'Well, all that's fine, but how do we fix Aurora's situation?'

Chaz paused for a moment. 'At the moment, they must be confused about who is helping her. We will use that to our advantage. No doubt they are still searching for her, so we let them find her.'

'What?' Maria yelped.

'Relax, we are not putting our newfound cousin at risk. Remember, we still have her car, and Desmond looks excellent in women's clothes.'

Aurora looked confused again. 'How will that help?'

Chaz replied, 'We stop hiding and go in the attack!'

# 39

Two days passed before the enacted their plan.

Aurora reluctantly agreed to stay with Monica and Diego. Chaz assured them he would keep them informed of their progress. The strategy he intended to employ was to confuse the guys they were dealing with. To that end, he had decided that he and Des, who would wear one of Aurora's tops and a scarf, would drive around in Aurora's car, knowing that it would eventually be spotted.

'What then?' Des asked.

When Chaz explained his plan, it brought a grin to Des's face. 'That should get their attention. Let's hope it works.'

It was the third day before they picked up a tail. 'Looks like we got a bite,' Chaz said as he spotted the Audi 8 in his rear-view mirror with a couple of tough-looking guys inside.

'About time. I have had enough of this dressing up,' grumbled Des from the passenger's seat.

'Sit still and try to look like a woman,' Chaz instructed, which got him a look that he could kill. 'Be quiet. I don't want them to think they have been spotted. We don't want them calling reinforcements. Not yet, anyway.'

So, for the next couple of hours, they led the Audi around the streets of Melbourne. The mobsters did their best to keep a distance from Chaz and his date, but eventually they found themselves on a stretch of road which led under a little-used underpass.

Suddenly Chaz jammed on his brakes, causing their tail to jamb on to avoid hitting them. Chaz quickly reversed up to the Audi. Where he promptly jumped out and ran up to the driver's door. The shocked driver did precisely what he expected. He wrenched the door open, trying to step out while reaching for the gun inside his jacket.

Big mistake! As soon as his hand was between the door jamb, Chaz kicked it with his considerable weight crushing the thug's hand. He could hear the bones crunch as the guy screamed in pain. At the same time, the other guy was attempting to get out to assist. When Des appeared holding up an object in his hand, he pointed it at the confused passenger, who was trying to figure out who this weird woman was.

With that, Des sprayed the guy with a strong-smelling liquid that blinded him. Simultaneously, he pulled the door open and started spraying the contents of the container into the interior, drenching the other guy, who was nearly unconscious from the pain.

The passenger screamed, 'Gasoline!' as Des shoved him back into the car.

Chaz roared from the other side. 'Don't move if you don't want to become a human torch. Just shut up and listen, and you might live.'

The guy on Des's side screamed. 'Don't!' in terror of being burnt alive.

'It's lighter fluid. But the same effect, and we did that was to get your attention. Have we got it?' He pointed to Des, who had a gas lighter in his hand that he was flicking on and off. The guy nodded furiously. 'Good,' continued Chaz. 'Now. Who is behind the attacks on our lady friend? And think carefully because we already know the answer. This is to test if you want to be burned alive.'

At this point, the other guy had recovered enough to discover their predicament. 'Don't do anything, Bogdan. We are covered in petrol,' his friend screamed.

'Lighter fluid,' Des corrected him. 'Answer the question,' he ordered, waiving the lighter as if to light it.

Bogdan began to blubber. 'We are part of the Yugoslav crew. Our boss is Yakov Milosevic. He told us to find the girl and bring her to him.'

Chaz glanced at Des. 'Wrong answer. You see, I was the one that stopped your pals that tried to kill her a few days ago.'

Des lit the flame and started to approach his guy, who began to scream hysterically. 'Do I give him one more chance?' he asked Chaz.

He did not have to reply. The other fellow started to answer frantically. 'Yes, we were supposed to kill her and make it look like a mugging. We were only following orders.'

'Did you people kill her father?' Des asked.

'Who?' asked the confused guy.

Chaz stepped in. 'That detective you killed was her father,' he snarled.

The one in the passenger's seat began to yell. 'We did not kill him. We covered up the mess the other crew made of the hit. All we did was burn his body,' glancing at the flame in Des's hand.

'Who are the other crew?' Chaz asked.

'Some crazy Chinese crew. It was them that insisted that that cop be taken out. They even used their assassin. Some crazy ninja chick. She killed him with her knife. The boss said we had to cover it up by burning him. He said it would create too much attention,' he blubbered.

'What is this person called?' Chaz asked.

'We never had anything to do with her. The boss was the only one that dealt with that mob of crazies.'

'Where can we find this Yakov?' Des asked.

The other one answered this time. He seemed to have recovered a bit. 'Nobody knows where he lives. He moves all the time. Most nights he spends in a club he has an interest in.'

Chaz spoke. 'Let me guess, The Odessa Club?'

The guy nodded in surprise. 'Who are you guys? Have you any idea whom you are messing with?'

Then Chaz decided to add a little intrigue to his plan. 'Yes, now we know exactly whom we are dealing with. As to who we are. We belong to an organisation that calls itself "The Umbrella Men".'

# 40

The roar of approaching cars at speed alerted them. 'Time to move. Their backup is arriving,' said Chaz as he slammed the door on his hapless victim.

Des did the same, waving the lighter at the terrified guy. 'If you guys try to get out of the car or if you try to follow us. I am placing this incendiary device under the car.'

Holding up a small box in the other hand. 'Any movement will activate the trembler switch, and boom!'

Spraying the door jamb with an extra squire of lighter fluid, he slammed the door. The brothers then ran to their car and took off. They knew exactly where they were going. They had picked the spot for their ambush carefully. A road that took them up and around was at the end of the cutting, leaving them with a clear view of what was happening down at the Audi parked below.

Two more Audi's roared up and screeched to a stop. Chaz grinned as they watched what was unfolding below. In the lead car, a blocky-looking character with a fearsome-looking bald head stepped out. Striding up to the car, he wrenched the door open.

'NOOOO!' came the scream from the guys inside.

The bald guy jumped back as he reacted to the stench of fuel and the anguished yell from inside the car. 'What's wrong? Why don't you idiots get out?' he screamed.

'We can't, Vlad. There is a bomb under the car. It has a trembler switch. It will go off if you move it,' Bogdan yelled.

Vlad signalled for one of his men to check it out. The guy moved in carefully and reached under the carrying out that package. Examining it, he stood up and announced loudly, 'It's only an empty tin.'

Up on the road above, Chaz nudged his brother. 'Trembler switch?' Des grinned.

'I thought it sounded good. Anyway, it worked. He believed me.'

Down below, the authoritarian-looking leader had opened the door again, but as Bogdan tied to clamber out with his wrecked hand, he pushed him back into this seat. 'Who did this?' he asked.

The guy gulped. 'The same people that took out the crew outside the club. They said they worked for some mob called The Umbrella Men,' he whimpered.

'What did they want?' he asked.

'They wanted to know who was behind the killing of that cop. But I told them it was not us and how we had to clean up the mess.'

Vlad leaned in and gripped his injured hand and began to squeeze. 'Now tell me exactly what you told them.' Through screams of torture, he and the terrified passenger told him everything. 'Okay, one last question, and I will let you out. Where were these guys from, and what did they look like?'

The passenger spoke first, 'They looked like Europeans, but they spoke with a funny accent. Not sure where he was from. Not American, but maybe Canadian?' he stammered.

Vlad stepped back. Then calmly lit a cigarette, then with the screams of the guys inside, he flicked the lit match inside and slammed the door.

Above, the brothers watched as the car erupted into flames, instantly incinerating the two guys inside. Chaz grunted, 'These guys are serious!'

The remaining gang members jumped into the cars and headed off without regard for their colleagues being burnt alive in the inferno. Chaz and Des followed them at a discrete distance and could see them joking and laughing as they drove.

After half an hour, the cars headed directly to a warehouse in the Docklands. As soon as they watched them enter, Chaz turned to his brother. 'Okay, we have seen enough. Now we have another location. I would bet that if we looked inside, we would find that Yakov character. Let's get out of here. We have stirred the pot enough for today.'

Des nodded in agreement as he drove away.

# 41

Inside the warehouse, Vladimir told his boss what had happened and how he had dealt with the failure.

'I hope those fools suffered. Letting themselves be caught like that. Did you find out anything before you disposed of them?' Yakov snarled at Vlad. He almost choked when Vlad told him they had talked about the Chinese and his connection to them. He started to rant and rave. 'Who are these people, and where did they come from? "The Umbrella Men"? I have never heard of them, have any of you?'

All he got was a shake of his lieutenant's head.

'Well, get out there and find them. Do you realise if word gets back to these crazy nut cases? It could derail this deal now that we are in the final stages. And put out the feelers. Somebody must know who these Umbrella pricks are.'

As Vlad hurried to follow his orders, Yakov headed into his small office, where he went behind his desk and pulled out a drawer, bringing out a silver tray brimming with white powder. Of late, his use of coke had gone through the roof. Ever since he had discovered what this crazy Chen Wah Yim had got him involved in. He shuddered in fear at the thought of anybody else learning his involvement.

When Chen approached him with his proposal to smuggle in some highly secret equipment, he first disregarded him as another fanatical nut. That was until he had placed a briefcase with half a mil on his desk.

'This is a retainer. If you can provide this service to my satisfaction, It will be followed by the balance of $3.5 million.'

He had not believed his eyes. Now he cursed himself for his greed for getting involved.

He hoovered up a monstrous line of the white powder. Sitting back, he recalled the day he related Chen's offer to Vladimir and his transport dilemma. Vlad was the one that produced the answer. It was in the form of one of their low-ranking soldiers that ran with the 'Nightshift' in the opal fields. When he brought him to the boss, he had a strange story to relate to him.

Years ago, he was running with a crew led by George Pratt. Somebody he feared and hated. That all changed one night. He was skulking around the claims to see if there was anything to steal when he spotted a miner. He was one of the foreigners that had recently fallen under Georges' grasp. When he saw him behaving strangely, he slinked into the shadows to watch.

The foreigner began loading all equipment and anything of value into a Ute at a frantic rate. He was just finishing when a woman appeared, presumably his wife. He could hear them talking in a foreign language, Spanish, he guessed. From what limited Spanish he could understand, the guy was screaming that they were finished with their partners and now they were getting out of town, taking everything they had with them. Hearing this, she began to become hysterical. She was crying that she would tell them what he was doing. She turned to march off, but before she had a chance, her husband grabbed her, putting his hands around her neck to try and shut her screams.

She struggled frantically as he squeezed harder. Finally, her struggles stopped. The Spaniard dragged the limp body over to an open mineshaft and dropped it in. Just then, George Pratt arrived. Seeing what had happened, he screamed, 'You have screwed up now. I will make sure you and your mate get what's coming to you! They will probably hang you.'

The Spaniard snapped. Picking up a shovel, he smashed George over the head, continuing to pummel him until it was pulp. Then he frantically jumped into the Ute and sped off.

Sensing an opportunity, the guy watching all this unfold ran back to his car and followed him. Three hours later, he found him kicking a flat tire at the side of the road. The Spaniard stopped what he was doing when he pulled up alongside him.

'Can you help me?' he choked.

The guy smiled. 'Sure,' he replied, then shot him in the head.

# 42

At that point, Yakov had gotten impatient. 'How is this of any help?' he asked his lieutenant.

Vlad turned to the guy who had put a bullet in the Spaniard's head. 'Show him.'

He did as he was instructed. He placed a weathered leather bag on the table and then tipped the contents onto the table.

'What is this?' Yakov asked.

Vlad picked four books from the pile of documents. They were passports. 'Handing one of them to Yakov, he said. 'Check out the name.'

Reading it, he said. 'Felipe Herrero. So, who is this?' Vladimir grinned. 'Only the owner of the largest transport company in the country. The puzzled look on his boss's face prompted him to continue. Turning to the guy, he pointed at the passports. 'Pick out the guy you shot that day.'

His henchman picked up Felipe's passport. 'This one.'

Then the penny dropped. Yakov turned to Vlad. 'Then who is running the company?'

Without replying, Vlad picked up Diego and Monica's passports. 'Well, if I was a betting man. I would say this pair.'

'How did you come across this guy?' he asked.

'I didn't. This guy figured it out himself. He spotted an article in the paper about the amazing success of this Spanish couple that had emigrated here and, after trying their luck at opal mining in Coober Pedy, came to Melbourne and built their empire.'

Yakov turned to the guy. 'Have you spoken to anybody else about this?'

The guy replied, 'No, I forgot about it until I overheard Vlad asking about some transport companies. So, I showed him this stuff.'

Yakov dismissed him, and as the guy left the room, he said to Vlad, 'Will you make sure that he is taken care of?'

This brought a smile to his face. Vlad answered. 'No problem, consider it done.'

Days after, they guy's headless body, minus his hands, were found floating in the Yarra River. After that, Yakov quickly found all the secretive owners' information using his contacts. Since then, everything seemed to be going smoothly. They had already delivered three packages, and the final one was due to arrive in a week. Then that inquisitive cop somehow established a connection between the Chinese and the Herrero transport and put a wrench in the works.

But that wasn't the worst of it. The thing that brought a cold shiver down his spine as he sat at his desk snorting another line was what he had just discovered. In error, one of his crew at the docks had opened the last package. He was Russian and could read the details of what it contained.

To his horror, the components included material that could be used to make a dirty nuclear bomb.

# 43

Chaz and Des put Aurora's car back in hiding and caught a cab to the Herrero's mansion, anxious to let their cousin know what they had discovered about her father's killer. Arriving, they knocked on the door, which was promptly opened by the butler.

'This way, gentlemen, they are awaiting you in the sitting room.'

Maria appeared, rushing up to them in excitement. 'I thought it must be you. Come on. I have a wonderful surprise,' leading them into the living room, where they stopped in their tracks. There assembled were all of Maria's family, including their brother Vincent. 'They arrived yesterday. When they contacted me from the airport, Monica and Diego insisted on sending a limo for them. Of course, when they arrived, they would not hear of them staying anywhere but with them.'

The next hour or so was taken up with the excitement of the grand reunion. Finally, Chaz drew his brothers, including Maria's dad, Bill, aside. 'Guys, we have a lot to catch up on, and things are starting to heat up. Des, will you bring Vin and Bill up to speed as best as possible, and I will speak to Aurora about the news on her father.'

While Des took them aside to tell them the strange events that had transpired since he and his brother had arrived, Chaz took her aside to fill her in on what they had discovered. After he had related what had happened and they discovered who the potential assassin was, Aurora hugged him. 'That is great news. Now we have a lead.'

He cautioned her. 'Don't get too excited. But you are right, and it is a start. Now let's join the others,' as they headed back to the emotional reunion of the Spanish family.

Later, while the ladies were arranging dinner, Chaz assembled the brothers, including Diego and Aurora, to plan their next move. By this time, Des had filled them in on all that had happened, including the incineration of the two guys in the car, which shocked the group.

'What kind of animals are these people?' Vincent retorted.

It was Bill that replied. 'The worst kind, all gangsters from that part of the world practice the worst kinds of violence. They make the Mexican cartels look like saints! The boys back in London had to resort in kind before a reluctant truce was called.'

It was Chaz that spoke next. 'I don't know about you guys, but this does not make much sense. First, if their object was to stop further investigation into the connection between this mysterious Chinese mob and you,' pointing at Diego, 'killing Aurora's dad in such a brutal manner and then trying and cover it up by setting him on fire could only draw more attention, not distract.' He got nods of agreement. 'Plus, if this Chinese group plans a terrorist attack, why would the authorities be trying to impede the investigation?'

Vincent answered. 'More questions than answers. As Sherlock Holmes would say, "A puzzle wrapped up in a conundrum," or something like that,' as he realised he had forgotten the correct saying.

Des added, 'And let's not forget. What are these guys bringing that they have resorted to blackmail? I can't believe it is simple machinery.'

With that, Maria informed them that dinner we ready. As they made their way to the dining room, Chaz noticed that Vincent was lost in thought. 'What up?' he asked.

'Not sure, let me think,' he muttered as they all regrouped for dinner.

## 44

Over dinner, some loose plans were formed. It was decided that more information was needed about this Yakov, and Chaz suggested he approach his friend, Gavin. With his connection to the Russians, he could help. Also, he decided he would contact their cop mate back in Adelaide the next day.

'So, what now? The evening is still young,' Des asked.

Chaz stood. 'I think it's time we guys went for a drink. At the same time, I can introduce you to The Amazing Gavin.' This brought some grumbling from the ladies, but they agreed to remain when he pointed out that it would not be safe for Aurora to be seen. 'Have you reached out to your father's partner yet?' he asked her.

'He texted me on that phone you lent me. He is anxious to help,' she replied.

'Good, keep yours silent until we figure out how to use it to our advantage. I suggest you text him and set up a meeting tomorrow.'

She nodded and then resumed the conversation with her new friends as she shared their fantastic stories.

Vincent pulled Chaz aside. 'I am going to stay here. you are better at that type of meeting.'

Chaz shrugged, but he knew his brother. 'What's up, something on your mind?'

Vincent was silent for a minute, then. 'Something about all this smells all wrong. Why would a Serb criminal enterprise be involved in a terrorist plot involving the assassination of a police officer? The last thing a crew like that would want is the type of attention it would bring.'

Chaz nodded. 'That's what s been bothering me. All I can think is they have got a mighty incentive.'

Vincent did not look convinced. 'No matter the reward, it is useless if you can't spend it. I have a strange feeling there is something else going on here. Don't forget that somebody in a position of power is impeding the investigation into a possible tourist attack. They would need a mighty good reason to do that!'

# 45

Police Commissioner Christine Wolfe snuggled into her lover.

'I needed to be with you tonight. The pressure from my superiors to resolve this terrorist threat, coupled with all the violence in the last few days, has made it very difficult to deflect the investigations. Whoever put those henchmen of Yakov's in hospital and the two more burnt to death in that car has ignited the press. Everybody is looking for answers. I don't know much how long I can contain this,' she groaned.

'Relax, my dear,' Stanford said, and stroked her hair. 'We only have to contain things for another ten days. Then it will be all over, and we can enjoy my success together.'

'Easy for you to say. Suppose my involvement in the death of that detective was discovered. I could spend the rest of my days behind bars, or worse.' She shivered at the thought of what she had done.'

'The final piece of equipment is arriving in the next couple of days. Then our Chinese friend can complete his plan.'

'Are you sure that he has no intention of injuring anybody?'

'Of course not. They only intend to create disruption,' he lied. 'Then the final part of our plan can be implemented. Soon I will be in a position to return this country to the glory days. No more dependence on others.'

Christine's phone beeped with an incoming text. 'Shit, they are looking for me. I will have to go. Can we meet again tonight?' she asked as she sprang from the bed, hurriedly getting dressed.

'Not possible, I'm afraid. I'm flying to Sydney. I have a meeting with Chen. We are going over the final details.'

He escorted her to the door, where an innocuous car waited, one that she used for her clandestine meetings. Kissing her goodbye, he returned to his study, glad that she was gone. Soon he would not have to put up with her incessant needs. Her purpose would have been served, and she would have to be dealt with. But that was a matter he could deal with later.

He lit a cigar, going over his plans and remembering how an innocent conversation with his lover had led him to Chen Wah Yim and his crazies. When she had revealed the possibility of a plot to stage a terrorist attack, he had disregarded it until she mentioned the possible involvement of the son of one of the wealthiest men in China and a favoured member of the Communist Party. He was supposed to be here to foster better relations at the behest of his father. But his intentions were the exact opposite.

Piquing his interest, Stanford reached out to his contacts and arranged a meeting with Chen on the pretext of providing government support for his father. They had met at his house and spent some time discussing his father's plans to foster better relations with the West. That is when he decided to act.

'I have to be honest with you, Chen. I invited you here tonight because it has come to my attention that we may have similar goals.' A puzzled look crossed Chen's face. 'Are you aware that you are under investigation for your involvement with the group called "Tsunami" that is suspected of planning a terrorist attack?' Chen could barely contain the look of shock on his normally inscrutable face. Stanford continued, 'No need to respond. You see, we have similar interests.' He then explained how he was in a position to deflect the investigation.

Eventually, Chen spoke. 'How would that be possible?' When Stanford outlined his plan, his said, 'Perhaps we do have a common goal.'

From that point, things had gone smoothly until his lady friend had slipped up, somehow leading this inquisitive detective to discover her involvement in suppressing the investigation. Then she had made the monumental blunder of trying to resolve the problem herself.

Since then, he had been trying to keep a lid on it until the plan was implemented. But that daughter of the cop and whoever was helping her had threatened to destroy everything. As he puffed on his cigar, he wondered, *Who are these people, and how are they causing all this trouble?*

# 46

Chaz and his entourage entered The Dogs Bar searching for The Amazing Gavin later that evening. He was seated in his usual spot. On sighting his friend, he signalled for them to head to the back room for some privacy.

After Chaz had introduced the group to him, he brought Gavin up to speed on all that had happened when drinks had been organised.

'That Yakov is bad news, but I am surprised he would be involved in terrorism.'

Chaz nodded. 'That was our thoughts. There must be a big incentive to risk the attention something like this would bring. I was hoping you could help.'

Gavin nodded. 'Sure, but not sure how I can be of assistance.'

'Actually, I was hoping your pal, Sergei, could help in that regard.'

Gavin looked puzzled. 'How?

'Well, when he was polishing off that couple of bottles of Vodka, from the conversation it seemed he had connections with the Russian Mafia.'

Gavin nodded. 'Continue.'

'Well, it would seem to me that if this Yakov were involved in such a venture, it would be sure to bring a massive response from the police. And, if I am correct, as far as they are concerned, Russian or Serb, or for that matter any Eastern Europeans involved in illegal activities, would suffer.'

'What do have you in mind?'

'What I would like is some pressure brought on him to explain his involvement with whoever this Chinese group is and whether he is aware of what they are planning.'

'Not sure if Sergei can help, but why don't we ask him?' He picked up his phone and, after speaking for a few minutes, he hung up, announcing Sergei was close by and on his way. 'Have you any other way of discovering who the Chinese mob is?'

Des put up his hand. 'I have an idea for that. We know that there will be another piece of equipment to be delivered soon. I reckon I should be the delivery guy.'

This brought a chorus of objections from the crew. 'Too dangerous. If anybody is doing that, it will be me,' Chaz snapped.

'Great idea, that way, if any of the crew involved in the attack on our cousin or, for that matter, the guys that burned their pals alive, should recognise you, they can return the favour.'

Just at that point, the monstrous figure of Sergei appeared. 'Where is the drink you promised me?' he roared.

Gavin ordered a bottle of Vodka from the barman and did the introductions. After they had explained what they had found out about Yakov possibly being involved in helping a terrorist group, they asked him what the repercussions would be if the Russians found out. Sergei just dragged his figure across his throat.

Chaz jumped in quickly. 'What we were hoping for was something other than cutting his throat. There is some pressure to find out what these Chinese are planning. We know there is one more delivery, which we understand is happening shortly. Des has put his hand up to drive it to their pickup point. Then with some luck, we can follow it and perhaps find out what they are planning.'

'Drink up,' Sergei instructed as he downed half of the bottle of Vodka.

'Where are we going?'

'To talk to Boris Semenov, and before you ask, he is the head of the Mafia here in Melbourne. I am sure he will be very interested in hearing your story.'

'Now?' Des asked.

'No time like the present. Let's go,' as he finished off the bottle.

# 47

Sergei's Mercedes wagon hurtled to its destination at breakneck speed, screeching to a stop in front of The Odessa Club, much to Chaz's surprise.

'I thought this was where the Serbs and Croats hung out?'

'I told you before. This is neutral ground. Somewhere all factions from our part of the world can go without fear of trouble,' he informed them as he jumped out, handing the keys to the valet and instructing him to keep them ready for him.

There was a different group of doormen at the entrance, but without hesitation they jumped to open it.

'Guess he is regular here,' Bill whispered as they made their way directly to the stairs leading to the private floors.

'Each gang have their own space,' Sergei informed them. 'But the Russian Mafia commands the top floor.'

Arriving on the upper floor, they we greeted by two enormous guys blocking the double doors to a suite. 'These guys are with me. They have important information for the boss that he will want to hear,' Sergei informed them.

'Just a second, I will tell him you are here,' one of them said as he stepped inside. A couple of seconds later, the doors burst open, and a tall, elegant gent emerged.

'Sergei, my monstrous friend.' Boris enveloped him in a bear hug, kissing him on both cheeks. 'What trouble do you bring to my door today?' He ushered him inside.

'My friend has some important information for you,' indicating his three friends.

Boris glared, then bursting out laughing, he waved. 'Come on, if you have survived his driving, you deserve a drink.'

The suite inside was surprisingly tasteful. The décor was modern and minimalist. Even the girls looked like they had stepped from the pages of *Vogue* magazine. After, they were seated and provided with drinks, Boris turned to his friend.

'Well, what is so vital that brings you here with these people?' he asked.

Sergei leaned in close and began to whisper in his ear.

His face froze. 'Clear the room.'

Like magic, the ladies and the guys sitting around stood and vanished into an adjoining room. When they were alone, Sergei told him what they had discovered. Boris said nothing until he had finished.

'How did you come by this information?' he asked.

'It would be better if my friend here explained,' Sergei responded, and gave Chaz a nod to speak.

Taking a deep breath, Chaz launched into the strange story of their attempts to find lost relations, which led them to discover how Yakov was blackmailing one of them to transport the mystery equipment for this "Tsunami" mob. He then told them of his run-in with Yakov's accomplices when they tried to kill his cousin.

Boris exploded. 'That crazy fool. If he is behind the killing of that policeman and, on top of that, being mixed up with some terrorist plot. When the cops discover his involvement, it will destroy all of us. He is a dead man!'

'Can I make a suggestion?' Chaz asked, trying to defuse the situation.

'What?' growled Boris, fixing him with a death stare. Even Sergei looked a little concerned.

'I agree he deserves whatever fate you decide, but if first you could find out what he knows about the plot, we can try to stop it before it happens. Also, discovering who assassinated my cousin's father would go a long way to appease the cops.'

He looked at the three guys as if they had just appeared, examining them individually. 'Who are you guys? What do you call yourselves?'

'We are just what I explained. My brothers, myself, and other family members are just looking for some relatives.'

He looked at them sceptically. 'Somebody who can take out three of his best men and succeed in getting two more burnt alive is not just some tourist. There is more to you guys than meets the eye.'

Des decided to have his say. 'Before the guys in the car got toasted, they asked the same thing. I came up with the name "The Umbrella Men" to create confusion.'

'I like you Irish guys, and I like your name,' he laughed. 'Okay, I will have a word with Yakov. You will have whatever information he has.'

Chaz hastily added, 'And with your permission, if he could be kept alive in case we need him. Would be much appreciated.'

He nodded. 'Agreed. Now for some Vodka, and you can tell me what you have planned.'

# 48

They stumbled out of The Odessa Club just as dawn was breaking, followed by Sergei, who seemed to be impervious to how much he drank. Piling into the car, Chaz gave him directions to the penthouse.

In what seemed moments, they screeched to a stop in front. The shaken passengers got out, and Chaz turned to thank Sergei, only to discover him getting out too.

'You did not think I was going to miss out on all this fun, did you?' he said, giving him a hefty slap on the back.

Up in the penthouse, Bill made some strong coffee while Sergei searched for the bar. They settled down to try and recover when his phone rang. It was Chief Inspector David George returning his call.

'Hello David, thanks for ringing me back. Our search has taken us in an alarming direction. I was wondering if I could come to Adelaide to discuss it with you?'

'No need, I am here in Melbourne. I had a few days off, so I hopped on a plane when I got your message. I figured something was up. I have some police business over here. Where are you?' he asked.

Chaz gave him the address, and the chief inspector he would be over as soon as he got a cab. Less than an hour later, he was standing in their living room, meeting everybody. When he saw Sergei, a puzzled look crossed his face.

'Don't worry, he is a friend,' Chaz assured him, and gave him a condensed version of all that had happened since they had last met.

'You must mean Detective James McCormack. I had the privilege of working with him and his partner, Alan Moffatt, when we worked on a case last year. His death was a tragedy. And now you tell me they are targeting his daughter? I had never met her, but he was proud that she had followed him and joined the police. What can I do to help?'

Chaz went on to tell him how the investigation into his death and the terrorist threat was being impeded and how he was convinced there was a mole on the inside. For that reason, she had tried to investigate on her own.

'I would like to speak to her.'

Concern crossed Chaz's face. 'She has lost all confidence in the authorities because of what has happened. I am unsure how she would feel about talking to you.'

'Tell her she would not be talking to the police. She would be talking to a friend of her father who would be just as anxious the bring the killer to justice.'

Nodding, he picked up the phone and called her, explaining what was happening. Then hung up. 'They are all coming over as soon as they can,' he informed them.

While waiting, Chaz related all that had happened in detail since they last met. The chief inspector then asked Sergei, 'Do you think your friends can get information from this Yakov guy without starting a gang war?

'We solve our problems in-house, Mr Policeman. The only one that had to worry is that clown, Yakov.'

They sized each other up for a moment, and Chaz wondered what he could do if these guys tangled. But he did not need to worry.

Sergei came over and, with a big smile, roared, 'Relax. These guys are my friends, and I can see you are a good guy. We can work together,' giving the chief inspector a friendly nudge.

When the others arrived, everybody got acquainted. The chief inspector went directly to Aurora. 'I am so sorry. Please call me David, not Chief Inspector. I knew your dad. He was a fine man. I hope together we can find the bastards that did this.'

Tears came to her eyes. 'Thank you, David. I remember Dad talking about you. He said they called you Rambo.'

David smiled and took her in his arms. When they had drinks in hand, everybody relaxed a bit. Des cracked a joke. 'We will need a much bigger place if we keep meeting like this.'

Not getting his humour, Monica stepped in. 'You no longer need this place, Chaz. It would be better if from now on you all stayed with us. As you know, space is not a problem at our home.'

'Des was only joking, Monica,' said Chaz. 'But there is much sense in what you say. But for now, let's decide on our next move.'

Diego spoke. 'I have news. They contacted us yesterday. The last package is arriving in two days.'

When Chaz heard this, he explained that they had decided that his brother would deliver the package, and then hopefully, we could follow it to its final destination.

'Who would follow it? They warned us there would be repercussions if that were to happen.'

It was the Russian that responded. 'That will not be a problem. I may be big, but back in Russia, I could follow a wolf to his pack and sit with them!'

Chaz stepped in. 'The problem is we still don't know anything about who these Chinese people are?'

Aurora sprang up. 'Remember, I have Dad's computer.'

'But you told us that there was nothing on it,' Chaz replied.

'I know, but Dad was good with computers, remember? He used to be in the Fraud Squad. He could find hidden files, and perhaps he hid something in his. From reading his notes, he was cautious because of his suspicions about an internal mole.'

'I can help with that. I have some experience in that department,' David added. 'Where is it?'

Aurora went to her backpack. 'Here, I haven't let it out of my sight since we were attacked,' handing it to him. 'Okay, I will take a look, and at the same time, I will reach out from my sources back at my home base to see what I can discover about this "Tsunami" mob.'

'Great, and Aurora, I think it is time we spoke to his partner. David assures us he can be trusted.'

She nodded in agreement. Des jumped in, 'Okay. Now it's time to create some mayhem!'

# 49

## THE SNOWY MOUNTAINS,
## NEW SOUTH WALES & VICTORIAN BORDER

Chen Wah Yim was in the office of his secluded property in the Snowy Mountains. Its ownership was well hidden as it had been purchased through several shell companies, which could not be traced back to him. Something he was now very glad of as he contemplated the disturbing news he had received from his man in the Croat gang.

When he had enlisted the help of Yakov, he had taken the precaution of bribing one of his men to keep him informed. The news that his attempts to silence the daughter of that inquisitive policeman had been foiled by some mystery group called "The Umbrella Men". His guy had told him how they had extracted the information from two of their men about the involvement of some Chinese people. But he assured him they were low-level players and did not know any details. Plus, they would not be speaking to anybody again, he had assured him.

Chen cursed to himself. He was close to fulfilling the plan he and his associates had dreamt up. His journey had begun as a young man attending cultural training. Something reserved for the children of the most influential people in China, and his father, Chen Guang, fitted that description perfectly. As one of the wealthiest people in the county, he was the owner of the largest industrial company, Xian Steel. Also, he was a staunch supporter of the Communist Party and was one of the leading proponents of fostering relations with Western nations. He believed the way for his country was to promote joint development and allow everyone to decide their own future.

A class friend had invited him one evening to a clandestine meeting of a few young men. They had a completely different agenda. They believed their country was going in the wrong direction, threatening the fabric of their culture. Like him, they all came from wealthy families, but compared with his father they were chump change.

Hence their reason for inviting him. Fortunately, he shared their ideology, as he was a firm believer in Chairman Mao's doctrines. Especially his most radical ideas. When his father had arranged for him to be attached to the Chinese Embassy here in Canberra, his political immunity allowed them to foster their radical plan of destroying any chance for the two countries to work together.

When he had solved the problem of how to import the components to assemble a low-yield nuclear device, which, to that point, was just a pipe dream, it suddenly became a reality. But when one of his idiot partners' loose lips threatened to undermine their plans, even his diplomatic immunity could not save him from planning a nuclear attack on one of the country's most important structures. If not for the approach by Cyril Sanford, the Deputy Prime Minister, informing him the anti-terrorist squad was investigating them, he had only just avoided being caught.

But Stamford had ambitions of his own. He explained that he could contain the authorities, and what he wanted in return would be a win-win for both of their aspirations. Except for the disastrous handling of the policeman's removal, everything had been going smoothly. Now he had to sort that out.

At that moment, Sun Yee On entered the room. She had been the one whose services he had called on to clean up the mess. 'You wanted to see me?' she asked.

Although Sun Yee On was the name he knew her by, he knew she went by many names. She was best known by the term "Shi no Tenshi", Angel of Death. To look at her, nothing would give the impression that she was anything more than a young Asian woman of medium build and height. The only feature that could hint at her true profession was her confident posture, and if you were to look into her coal-black eyes, it was like looking into a bottomless pit.

She was an assassin and considered one of the best. If she undertook the hit, regardless of what happened, that person was dead.

He turned to her avoiding her stare. Then said, 'We have a problem.'

# 50

As Yakov entered the club, he immediately noticed something was wrong. The guys at the door had avoided eye contact, but before he could react, a guy stepped up to him.

'Mr Semenov would like to speak to you,' pointing to the stairs. His look conveyed that a refusal was not an option.

Recovering his composer, he gave the guy a nod. 'Lead the way.'

As soon as he entered the suite, he knew he was in trouble. The usual crowd were missing and in their place were some grim-faced leaders of the different Eastern European factions. Boris Semenov was standing facing him. As the Russian Mafia were considered the pack leader, Boris was the accepted representative for all the people in the room.

'To what do I owe the pleasure of this audience?' Yakov asked defiantly.

Boris pointed at a couch. 'Take a seat.'

Yakov nodded and settled into one of the chairs. If not for the fact that he was confident that he was safe within the confines of this club, he would have expected to be carried out of here in small bags.

Boris began to speak. 'Some alarming news had reached our ears. Your clan has been aiding a terrorist group of Chinese origin planning an attack on this country.'

Yakov jumped to his feet. 'Who is telling these lies?'

'Sit down!' Boris roared. 'You don't ask the questions here. You answer them. Now stop denying what we already know. What we want from you is exactly who these people are and what you transported for them.' As Yakov went to protest again, Boris raised his hand to silence him. 'I am not finished. What were you thinking killing that police officer and then burning him?'

Before he could respond, Yakov felt something slipping around his neck. He knew instantly what it was, a garrotte!

'Just because you are under the safety of this place, we can still have you outside before you stop breathing. So be sure that what you say is not your last,' Boris warned him.

Knowing he had no choice, Yakov began to speak. 'It is true I moved some machinery for some Chinese guy. He assured me it was only scientific components for which the Australian government required a special permit,' he spluttered, feeling the cord tightening.

'Who is this Chinese guy, and what exactly did you transport?'

'He said his name was Chen. As to what was in the packages, I have no idea. He arranged for them to ship to Australia then I would arrange to clear customs. I have a contact tha…'

'Stop. Boris snapped. 'We know about your blackmail scheme. We want the Chinese and the location of the "components" you transported.'

Yakov nearly passed out. *How did they find out about Herrero transport?* he thought as he felt his breathing getting cut off. 'Please, I can't breathe. Let me explain,' he gasped.

Boris gave a barely perceptible nod, and he felt the cord relax. He then explained the appearance of this mysterious Chen and how he was about to disregard him until he produced the case full of money. He pleaded that he was assured the packages were not guns or explosives, and judging by the size of the boxes he did not see a problem.

'So let me get this straight. Some stranger asked you to move some packages based on his assurance that they were not "dangerous" plus their size. You then went ahead?' Yakov nodded, and Boris roared, 'You greedy idiot! The money blinded you. Did you not question how a foreigner knew how to locate you when you are constantly moving around? I will tell you why, because he had help. Powerful help. *Durak.* Fool.' He paused, then said, 'Why was this policeman killed, and who ordered the hit?'

Yakov nearly expired. 'I swear I had nothing to do with that. I have no idea who was behind it,' he lied. 'Maybe it was Chen?'

Boris stared at him intensely. 'How do you contact this Chen?' he asked.

Yakov shook his head in despair because he had no idea how to get the guy. As long as the money kept coming, he preferred the be in the dark. He was cursing his stupidity and greed that was now about to get him killed.

'Take him to the other room, we need to talk,' Boris ordered.

Yakov was marched away, convinced that he had signed his death warrant. For what seemed like an eternity, he sat waiting on his sentence. Then the door opened, and he was escorted back in front of his peers.

Boris spoke. 'Here is what has to happen if you continue living past this moment. You will bring to us the location of this Chen and whatever was in those packages. And also the assassins of that policeman. Before you plead, remember that your life depends on your answer.'

Yakov did not hesitate, hardly believing that he might leave this place alive. 'Yes, I will make my best effort.'

'In case you had any idea of running, you know our reach. You are a walking dead man until you fulfil these requests. Better hurry, the clock is ticking.'

As he was escorted out of the club and into the open, Yakov's brain was churning, trying to figure out how he could save his miserable life.

# 51

Sergei was ushered straight into the sitting room as soon as he arrived at the Suarez mansion. Everybody, it seemed, had taken Monica's offer of ample accommodation plus substantial security.

'I have news,' he announced.

Desmond jumped up. 'Great work. Grab a drink. We are just waiting for the chief inspector to arrive. He has news also.'

As if waiting to be announced, the man strode into the room, followed by an older gent. He was at least 6' 6" and, at a guess, would top the scales at over 120 kilos, most of which had accumulated around his waist.

'Alan!' Aurora screamed, and threw her arms around his massive neck. He effortlessly lifted her off the ground. 'I am glad you are here.'

'Well, my old pal called and filled me in on what was happening. Wild horses could not have stopped me.'

Aurora turned. 'Everybody, this is my dad's partner, inspector Alan Moffatt,' then hugging him again as he tried to wave at the crew.

While everybody was getting acquainted, drinks and food were served. David explained how he had reached out to Alan, and that he realised they would need his help accessing information on the quiet.

Chaz stopped the chatter. 'Sorry, but I think we should get started. Sergei, you have news?'

Sergei filled them in on the information they had extracted from Yakov and the tasks he had undertaken.

'Well, at least we have a name, Chen, but not much else.'

'We can help with that,' Alan replied. 'We have cracked the code on James' laptop, and Chen's full name is Chen Wah Yim. He is the son of one of China's richest and most powerful men. From what I can decipher from his notes, James believed the son was operating without his father's knowledge.'

'Why didn't Dad pull him in for questioning?' Aurora asked.

'A couple of reasons. First, he has diplomatic immunity. He is attached to the Chinese Embassy. Bringing him in for questioning as a cultural attaché would need firm evidence. That's where it got weird when he took it to his superiors. He got pushback from the highest level. All he kept getting asked was who his informant was. Something he wouldn't or couldn't divulge. That's when he began to suspect something was rotten. He was convinced the department had a mole. From what I could see in his notes, he suspected somebody at a very high level.'

'Did he say who?' Chaz asked. Alan shook his head. 'Then we will have to find out more about this, Chen.'

Vincent Savage QC announced from the back of the room, 'His name, as you say, is Chen Wah Yim, although he sometimes uses the name Guang and was educated in the finest European schools. As the son of the country's most influential and wealthiest men, he was being groomed for some high office. He was recruited by the radical group when attending cultural education. His primary attraction to them was his access to money. But he quickly became radicalised to their aims. Like many children with an influential father figure, they often feel insignificant, especially as he was the second son. Whatever the reason, he became deeply involved. It would have stopped there, just talk and bluster, if not for his meeting with a son of a Russian arms dealer and his father sending him to Australia to further his education. It would appear that his father has no idea of his involvement with this group.'

# 52

Chaz was surprised to hear Vincent speak. Since his arrival, he and Bill had kept to themselves. He just assumed that they were dealing with their numerous business interests.

'Vince, how'd you get this information?' he asked.

'You know I never reveal my sources, or I should say, we,' nodding to Bill. 'But we can tell you that this group he is supposed to be connected to, "Tsunami", is creating some chatter. Up to lately, it was just like hundreds of this type of splinter groups that spring up. Almost all of them never do anything but talk. That was until these guys hooked up with a very unscrupulous arms dealer called Alexander 'Sasha' Smirnov. That's when things get a bit hazy. The chatter is that they were supplied with some, and I quote, "Frighting material", but so far, no word of what that could be or their intended target.'

David, as the chief inspector now insisted everybody call him, jumped in. 'That would agree with the information James received from what we could decode from his notes and what he had stored on his laptop.'

Des stepped in. 'So where does this leave us?' he asked.

'Okay. The last package has arrived, and Diego will hand walk it through all the paperwork,' Chaz answered, glancing at him for approval.

Diego replied. 'Providing everything goes smoothly, I will have it here for you guys to examine before we deliver it.'

Chaz continued. 'That's only if we can check it without being discovered. Then Des and Sergei take over. Des will deliver the package to the drop-off point. It is a much-visited tourist stop called 'The Dog on the Tucker Box'. It's the perfect place to make the drop. It is always busy. Lots of petrol stops and restaurants. At this point, what happens from what Diego has told us, Des just stops and waits until somebody picks up the package. Then Des has to wait for one hour before moving. He will be watched.'

'So how do you follow them?' Aurora asked.

'That's where Sergei comes in. He will be following Des. As soon as they collect it, he will pick up Des, and they will follow the package,' he replied.

'But won't they spot you?' she asked.

'Thanks to David, we will have a tiny transmitter attached to the package. It doesn't have a great range, but we can follow from a distance.'

'Looks like we have a starting point,' Des added.

Vincent stood. 'I have a few questions and suggestions, or rather, demands.' This got everyone's attention. 'First question. Could that tracking device be traced back to you?' he asked David.

David shook his head. 'No way. Anybody can buy one from Radio Shak.'

'Good. Because from this point, you three,' indicating David, Alan, and Aurora, 'are law officers and, in the eyes of the courts, have to abide by stringent rules regarding how you collect evidence, correct?'' They were nodding. 'I know my brothers. Chaz did not get that scar on his face shaving. And how Desmond is not locked up or dead is beyond me. So, from this point on, you three will have to operate behind the scenes.'

Aurora jumped up. 'But I want to help.'

Vincent fixed her with a glare. 'Okay, a question. What if what these guys have planned to break the law, which it will, knowing them? If you help and it goes to court, will you lie under oath?'

She just dropped her head.

'Good. Now, if you allow me to oversee the plans, I can insulate you three from any wrongdoing when it comes time to take these people, whomever they are. Your character cannot be called into question.'

There was silence. He paused for effect as if he was presenting to a grand jury.

'Where are you getting all this information? From what David and Alan have discovered, it would appear that the snitch contacted him. Why?' Chaz asked.

'We asked ourselves the same question when we went looking for information. It was like somebody was feeding us clues.' Before Chaz could interrupt, he continued, 'And who in a well-run police system as exists in this country would have the power and ability to smother a possible terrorist attack? The mole is in a position of great power. But no matter how we have looked at it, none of it makes sense. We believe there is another agenda being orchestrated by an even higher authority.'

Everybody started to ask questions at once. But over the chatter, the booming voice of David spoke. 'There is something else we discovered on his laptop. The night he was murdered, he had a meeting arranged with the person he believed was the mole!'

# 53

The next morning, Vincent decided that David, Alan, and Aurora would remain with him and Bill. They would continue investigating behind the scenes to uncover more about Chen and his mob. Knowing that perhaps James had met with the mole opened the possibility that they were his killer. David and Alan disagreed.

'Snitches are usually low-hanging fruit. They are not the type to murder a high-ranking policeman.'

'Okay. While you guys are following leads from your end, Bill and I will try to make more sense of the notes and files on his laptop.' They both agreed, but Vince could see the reluctance on Aurora's face. 'Sergei, could I speak to you?'

'How can I help?' he boomed.

Vince winced. 'Could you reach out to your friend, Boris? Perhaps he could use his influence to find out what that arms dealer, Sacha, supplied these guys?'

He nodded. 'I will call him now so he can get on it while helping with the package delivery,' he declared, obviously enjoying his new position.

When they assembled for breakfast the next morning, it was easy to see that nobody looked like they had a wink of sleep except for Des. He loved this. The more risk, the happier he seemed to be. But by the expression on Maria's face was a source of concern for her.

Diego entered carrying what looked like a midsized suitcase, which appeared to be metal. They gathered around while David and Alan examined it. 'No chance of opening it,' said David. 'It is protected with combination locks. If we interfere with it, we could alert them that we are trailing them.'

'Okay. Let's get on with it. It's at least five hours from here to the drop-off place,' Des urged, excited to be in action.

Chaz called for attention. 'This is the plan. Des will drive to the drop-off point, and I will follow behind to pick him up. Sergei, you will go with Des to drive the car back. If we leave it there, it could alert them.'

Sergei almost exploded. 'What? No. You will need me when the shit goes down. I am not a chauffeur.'

Diego stepped in. 'He is right. They are used to me delivering the package. I will drive. That way, Des can remain hidden until you pick him up.'

Chaz nodded in agreement. 'Okay. Sergei, you are with me.'

'Right at last. Now can we get this show on the road?' Des demanded.

# 54

Six hours later, an exhausted Diego pulled into the parking lot of The Dog on the Tucker Box. He had hardly slept for the last two days as he transported the package through all the departments. When he had asked why he could not do the delivery alone, Chaz was quick to point out that these people had killed already. There was no way they were going to let him go alone.

'Stay down out of sight until they retrieve the suitcase. They usually only take a short time,' he said to Des, who was hidden behind the seats, covered by a thick blanket.

After what seemed to Des to be hours, he heard the door open. No words were exchanged, only the sound of the case being picked up and the door closing. A minute later, the sound of an Audi 8 pulling alongside alerted him to Chaz's arrival.

'They are here. I will turn off the interior lights, slide out the back door, and stay down. Good luck, my friend,' Diego whispered.

As he heard the door open quietly, Des slipped out, shutting the door, and transferred into the back of the Audi. Diego sighed, sitting back to grab a nap before he was allowed to leave.

Chaz was driving while Sergei followed the signal from the transmitter. 'How is the signal?' asked Des from the back seat.

'Perfect,' he replied, pointing to the map they were following on his laptop.

'Where are we going?' he asked.

'Too soon to tell. We are heading north, climbing into the Snowy Mountains, it would seem,' he replied.

They carried on, meandering through the winding roads up into the mountains. 'We seem to be heading towards Kosciuszko National Park,' Sergei commented.

'What's there?' Chaz asked.

'Not sure. Some snowfields in the winter but very little activity at this time of year. Only nature lovers,' he replied.

They continued for another couple of hours when Sergei reacted. 'They turned onto a private road. It seems to lead to some estate.'

They stopped at the bottom of the road. 'Looks like we are stopping. We will have to walk from here,' Chaz said.

They parked the car on the street outside and started up the path. It was already dark, but they had brought torches. They walked about two kilometres before the gates of a large estate came into view.

'What now?' Des asked.

'All we can do is watch,' Chaz replied, and looked around. 'Let's climb up,' pointing to a steep rise that overlooked the place.

From there, they could see behind the walls. A hacienda-type house occupied a large area, including a helipad with a Bell helicopter parked at the front of the property.

'Somebody has money,' Des whispered as they observed from behind some bushes.

The house was surrounded by a large veranda that prevented them from seeing any activity inside. Chaz had just about to leave when they heard the chopper spool up. 'Hold on. Someone is leaving.'

Then from the house appeared two men. One was a short person of Asian appearance striding to keep up with the pace of the other gent. He was tall, well over six feet, and walked with the confidence of someone that was used to being followed.

*That must be Chen. But who is the other guy?* he mused.

The tall guy seemed to be issuing instructions to Chen. Then turned and climbed into the helicopter. As it lifted, Chaz slid back out of sight of the house. 'Okay, we have seen enough. Time to go.'

'Are we following it?' Sergei asked, pointing at the chopper.

Chaz and Des just looked at each other, then Des replied, 'Haven't figured out how to fly yet, Sergei.'

He just nodded and followed them back to the car. They failed to notice the motorbike in the distance behind them as they drove off.

# 55

Chen Guang returned to his secluded estate as the Cyril Stanford helicopter disappeared into the clouds.

This had been their final meeting before the implementation of their plans. With the arrival of the final components, they had discussed the timing of the events that would deliver the 'Tsunami's' message that would cripple this country's and his father's hope of normalising relations with the West.

The second phase of the plan, and the reason for Cyril's involvement, was designed to place him as Prime Minister. It was in the capable hands of the assassin, Sun Yee On.

When this inquisitive cop discovered who the police informant was, and they had made matters worse by trying to solve the problem themselves, Cyril had reached out for his help.

Luckily, he had already reached out to his contacts back in China for an assassin to carry out the final phase. When she arrived, he had asked her to clean up the problem of this inquisitive cop. Still, when she reported back with disturbing news, he decided to use that fool Yakov. But his desire to burn everything only worsened matters.

The resulting publicity had almost destroyed their plans, but Cyril's insider had managed to contain things until the emergence of a new threat from these mysterious "Umbrella Men".

Whomever they were, they seemed to be well informed. He was thankful he had not disclosed the deadly weapon he intended to release. Despite questions from Cyril and even Sun Yee On about his intentions, he had convinced them that he planned to destroy some major infrastructure in the Snowy Mountains. He knew if anybody discovered his real intentions, they would never agree to such drastic measures.

Entering his office, he found his fellow conspirators gathered and inspecting the last components of the device. 'Is everything in order?' he asked.

They sprang to attention. The one called Cui Guozhi answered. 'All good excellency. We have everything necessary to prepare the glorious device,' turning to the other two.

'The electronics have been tested and functioning perfectly,' his partner, Ding Fan, replied.

Then the one most crucial to the mission spoke. Dai Huang was in charge of the vital component. 'The fissionable material is stable and ready for assembly,' he announced proudly.

'How long until you have it assembled and ready for use?' he asked.

Guozhi replied, 'We are about to transport all the components to the designated site for assembly. It will be ready for detonation within a few days.'

'Have you calculated the effect?'

'The detonation will decimate the surrounding area for about 2 to 3 kilometres and result in the collapse of one of the dams. Also, the contamination carried in the water supply to the farmlands in central NSW and Victoria will disrupt the food supply for years. The effect on the economy will be disastrous.'

'Good. Now go and prepare the task of changing the direction of our glorious country and setting it on the path to restoring the old dynasty.'

They bowed and then hurried to complete their task.

Chen sat to consider the final stage, which made him wonder, *Where is Sun Yee On?*

# 56

The assassin crouched behind the screen of her BMW S1000RR motorbike, keeping her distance from the car she was following. She had observed them on one of the remote cameras that dotted the estate and had decided to follow.

After they had taken the main road to Melbourne, she decided to take care of another problem. She pressed a button on her encrypted satellite phone, which was immediately answered. In her headset, she heard a voice ask, 'How can we help?'

'I will need my equipment available in Melbourne. The usual place.'

The voice replied, 'It will be available by morning,' then disconnected.

The car she was following turned into a familiar estate. She stopped. This was something she had not expected. Had the Herrero's solicited aid? She did not think this old couple would take the risk, considering what Yakov had hanging over their head. It added another dimension to her task.

Starting the bike, she headed to her hideout in the city. Located in the Docklands, it was an old warehouse that had been converted into a loft apartment. The automatic door opened as she pulled the bike inside and parked it beside a late-model BMW 7 Series. Then she took the lift to the converted loft above. She checked to see if all her alarms were untouched. Entering, she went to see if her request had arrived. Her requirement was stacked in the corner. Satisfied, she headed for the shower to clean the road grime off from her long trip.

Sun Yee On, whose real name was Li Yang, reflected her mixed race. With a Japanese father and a Chinese mother, which both races frowned upon, it made her an outcast in both countries. If she had been a male in feudal Japan, she would have been called a 'Ronin', a Samurai without a master. But thanks to her father's teaching, she had learned remarkable skills as an assassin, which broke down those barriers when her unique talents were called upon.

After the shower, she dressed and made herself something to eat. She began to prepare for the task at hand. Opening the packages, she spread them on a large table and assembled them. She first took the pistol, a Beretta model 71, one she favoured. With silencer, the sound was little more than a polite cough. Yet the results in her hands were always lethal. After it was assembled, she checked the action. She started on the sniper rifle. The SAKO TRG 42, manufactured in Finland, used a 300 Winchester Magnum round. With a range of 1100 metres, it would be perfect for the assignment she had undertaken.

Within a second, she was sound asleep, unfazed by her deadly work ahead.

# 57

Yakov made his way upstairs to a meeting he had been called to by Boris. He had no choice but to comply. He had brought his sidekick, Vlad Stalin, along with him. He wanted to assure Boris that he was doing everything to get answers. Vlad was Russian, and he hoped that would help.

Boris was sitting behind his desk. 'Before you say anything and get yourself killed by lying, I am going to tell you what I know. I know the name of your Chinese friend. He is Chen Wah Yim, a diplomat at the Chinese Embassy. He is untouchable. You moron.' Before Yakov could open his mouth, he continued, 'We have located the arms dealer that supplied your friend with the so-called harmless machine parts. He has informed us that one of the parts is a triggering mechanism that could be used to construct a dirty bomb. He also informed us that you have delivered enough fucking plutonium to flatten a two kilometre area.'

Yakov froze on the spot. But the expression on Vlad's face caught Boris's attention. Yakov burst out. 'I had no idea what he was carrying. I had no contact with whoever was supplying him.'

'What do you know that makes it worth keeping you alive?'

Yakov thought franticly. 'When he contacted us to clean up the mess his assassin had made, he let slip that she was already here for his plan.' He was flustered. 'He said not to worry about that. Just cover up the cop's death.'

'And the best you could come up with was burn him in his car?' he asked.

Yakov reacted by pointing at Vlad. 'He can explain. I sent him to take care of it.'

Boris stood. 'Get him out of my sight,' he ordered to his head guy. 'Alive, I might want to kill him myself.'

Ask Yakov was marched out, Vlad awaited his fate. 'You are Russian?' Boris asked. Vlad nodded. 'Then I have to assume you are cleverer than that idiot.'

Again, a nod. 'So, what can you tell me about this botched whack job?'

Vlad began, 'I first knew about it when he asked me to clean it up. He said this Chinese guy had sent his lady assassin to do it, and it had gone badly.'

'So, what did you see?'

'That whoever had killed this guy was no killer. The guy had been stabbed in the neck, in the jugular vein. It was messy. The instrument must have been jagged because it ripped the wound open when he struggled. He would have been unconscious in seconds.'

'So why burn him?' Boris questioned.

'I was told to cover up the mess. I assumed they did not want his method of death disclosed. The car was in a deserted part of the Docklands. I would guess the meeting was a secret one.'

Boris paused to think. 'You seem to be a smart guy. You can guess you will need a new employer very soon, yes?' He did not wait for a reply. 'Here is what I propose. Stick with that idiot. See if you locate where this Chen is operating from. It is not any of his known addresses. So don't waste your time there. Do you agree?'

Vlad replied. 'As you have said, I am not stupid. Of course, I want to help. This idiot could have put us all in danger.'

'I have asked the guy that supplied the stuff what the chance of them being able to assemble an effective device is. He said it was remote. A dirty bomb has never been used successfully, even by the military,' he said.

Vlad was not so sure, but agreed nonetheless. He already had an idea of how to locate this Chinaman. He intended to keep it to himself because he was sure he would become as redundant as his boss as soon as he disclosed it.

# 58

As soon as Yakov entered his apartment, he sensed something was wrong. All of the locks were undisturbed, but the air circulating alerted him. Before he could react, a voice came from the darkness.

'I opened a window. It was a bit stuffy. I hope you don't mind?'

A light clicked on, illuminating an Asian-looking girl that looked like a college student. Except for the pistol pointing at his chest, and her coal black eyes.

'Take a seat. I want to discuss some things with you. Do you know who I am?' she asked.

He sat nervously. 'I would assume you are in the employ of Mr Chen.'

'Very good. And what service do you think he has engaged me for?' He swallowed, afraid to answer. 'I will help you. He has engaged me in assassinating a high-ranking member of the country's government. Now, I know you did not do the dirty work, but I am sure the way the policeman was dispatched was described to you. Do you know who I am?' she asked. He shrugged negatively. 'The name you may know me by is 'Shi No Tenshi' or to translate, Angel of Death.'

He shuddered. He had heard that name whispered in fear. When she took a contract, that person would die.

'I see you recognise the name, so having heard how the policeman was dispatched, do you think this was my handiwork?'

He shook his head vigorously. 'No. Vlad said this was the work of an amateur,' he blubbered. 'It was Chen who asked us to clean up. We just assumed it was his work.'

She nodded. This fool had no idea what he had got himself mixed up in. 'Have you got a car here?' she asked. He nodded again. 'I want you to take me to where he was killed,' indicating for him to move.

Twenty minutes later, they parked where the burnt-out car had been discovered. He had driven to the correct location. She knew this because she had previously been where the policeman and the informant had met. This mysterious Englishman had tipped off Chen, who had gone to the pains to keep his identity a secret from everybody. He had asked Chen to intervene as the snitch was becoming very nervous.

So, Chen had asked her to observe the meeting and resolve it discreetly. That was when she saw the passenger attack the policeman. He had been taken entirely by surprise and slumped into unconsciousness almost at once. His assailant did not wait to see the outcome, bolting from the car like a scared rabbet into the night. When Li inspected the scene, it was evident from the jagged wound that this was a panicked attack.

Yakov speaking brought her back to the present. 'What now?' he asked.

She opened the door of the car and stepped out. Then leaning in, she replied, 'We are finished.' She quickly raised the silenced Beretta and gave him two shots to the head.

She was not concerned with any trace, but to create the illusion of a gang-related hit, she attached a piece of clothing to a length of wire and dipped it in the petrol tank. She lit it and tossed it into his lap when it was soaked. She watched the car and Yakov go up in flames, wondering what direction this strange assignment would take next.

After Chen had approached her with the contract to assassinate a leading politician, she was approached from a surprising direction. Someone from the highest reaches of the communist party had suggested she take the assignment. She pointed out that when she took a job, she always carried out. They said they understood and offered a suggestion. They explained this and said they wanted to discover what Chen and his pals had planned. They did not want her to intervene. If she found anything, inform them of what they were planning. They said that they would handle it from there.

She would not have considered it, but she undertook what they requested because the request had come from a source that piqued her curiosity. When she reported the identity of the cop's killer, she was asked to discover the connection and what made them take such risks. She balked at first. She never asked the reason for her assignments. But for some reason, in this case, she was breaking that rule.

Pondering her next move as she made her way home.

# 59

Sergei hurried into the sitting room where they were all gathered, digesting the news from their discovery of the package's destination and planning their next move.

'I have just spoken to Boris. He discovered what the Chinese were transporting. The guy that sold the stuff to Chen has been convinced to speak.'

The way he said that left no doubt that he had told the truth.

'Stuff to make a nuclear bomb,' Desmond yelped. 'Why would that crazy guy sell stuff like that to some fanatics? What did he want to do, start World War 3!'

Sergei put his hand up. 'He was asked that, and he told us that this stuff was readily available from defunct Cold War sites, discarded since the end of the collapse of the USSR. Getting the stuff is not hard. Getting it to function is nearly impossible without military help. Even then, no type of nuclear device had ever been successfully used. I have been told that a dirty bomb used as a premise in many movies has never been successful in real life.'

'I am sure you will understand if we don't take that information at face value. David, Alan, surely this requires police action?' Chaz asked.

Vincent began to speak. 'Easy to say, but remember all we have is the word of an arms dealer and the head of the Russian mafia. With due respect, Sergei, if the boys take that to their superiors, the first thing they would be asked is where the evidence is. That's even without the intervention of the informant. Right now, we have the advantage. We are the only ones who know these guys' location and a probable site for the attack if there is one. This information is something only we can act on, Chaz,' he said, handing over to his brother.

Sergei again jumped, explaining how Boris had turned Yakov's second in command, giving him the task of locating Chen. He left no doubt as to Boris's intentions if they discovered them.

'Then we have to act. We must find out if this is a serious threat of just some cranks spinning wheels,' he replied.

Vince nodded in agreement. 'I would not assume that these are some fanatics with too much money and time on their hands. They're getting help from some powerful people. I am convinced there is a second agenda here, but we have no idea what it is.'

Just then, Aurora let out a shriek. 'Look!' pointing at a special news broadcast on the television.

The announcer was at a crime scene. In the background was the burnt-out shell of a car. Police and crime personnel surrounded it. The announcer explained that the vehicle was registered to a known criminal named Yakov Milosevic. They recovered a wallet that identified the burnt corpse as him.

'That's where Dad was discovered,' she cried.

The bulletin continued. 'A police officer said it was gang retaliation for the murder of Chief Detective James McCormack in a similar manner. The case was ongoing.'

She exploded. 'Liars. Nothing has been done. This is a coverup.'

Alan went to comfort her while, at the same time, Chaz turned to Sergei. 'Is this Boris's work?'

Sergei shook his head. 'He told me he was keeping him alive if he needed to use him. In any case, he would not have given him such an easy death,' he said.

Des gave Chaz a bang on the shoulder. 'Look. There is that guy!' he shouted. He was pointing at the TV. The reporter had cut to another location and interviewed a tall, elegant gent.

'Minister, has the government any comment about this escalation of criminal violence?'

He replied in a dulcet cultured accent. 'I have expressed my concern to our Prime Minister in this regard. The influx of refugees and immigrants from these lawless nations threatens our nation. If unchecked, I believe It could even lead to domestic terrorism.'

The reporter quickly responded. 'Does that mean that you disagree with his policies?'

'Please don't try to twist my words. I was pointing out that escalation is of great concern, and I am sure the Prime Minister has the same concerns. He has my full support,' as he terminated the interview.

Des reacted. 'Who is that guy?'

David answered. 'He is the Deputy Prime Minister and the Minister in charge of the police. His name is Cyril Stanford. Why?'

'He was at the exact location that the package went to. We saw him leaving. He had a helicopter. Chen was speaking to him as he was leaving. It appeared as if this guy was issuing instructions. We couldn't hear anything.'

Alan chipped in. 'He is an ex-Brit. Very wealthy from all accounts. Probably his private helicopter, I would imagine. A bit of a mystery man, not married and quite the man about town. He and Michael Parker, the Prime Minister, are reputed not to get on. Not surprising considering their socially different backgrounds.'

'All fascinating and certainly worth investigation. We will take care of that,' Vincent said, indicating to his crew. 'David, Alan, and Aurora, can you check out the connection? Remember, Chen is a diplomate attaché, and there might be a perfectly reasonable explanation for their meeting.'

Des mocked. 'Sure, and pigs can fly.'

Chaz intervened. 'Sound good to me. At the same time, while you try to find out what this guy has to do with all of this, Des, Sergei, and I will go to New South Wales and try to discover what these guys are up to.'

'How do you plan to do that?' Aurora asked.

'What we do best. The unexpected,' he replied.

# 60

Chaz, Des, and Sergei had been back at the Snowy Mountains for two days. They had acquired accommodation in the nearby town of Thredbo, a popular skiing resort in the winter. At this time of the year, they had the place almost to themselves. The only people that came at this time of the year were campers and hikers. This gave them the perfect cover to explore the surrounding of his estate.

They discussed what they had observed since they arrived, which had little so far. Chen had not left the estate, although they saw him outside talking to a couple of other Asians. The staff came and went daily, and Des managed to start a conversation with the gardener in the local tavern. He did not have much to offer.

'Ignorant pricks. They barely speak to us. Only to bark orders,' he complained as he took another free drink from Des. 'He and his three pals only talk in some weird language. If he didn't pay so well, and in cash,' he added with a wink, 'I would be out of there tomorrow.'

'That's all I could discover without raising his suspicion,' Des said to Chaz. 'I managed to find out that he had no guards. The gardener said the only people he had seen were three guys and an Asian girl. But she had been gone for the last few days.'

Chaz nodded. 'Good work. We have been researching the area for a possible target. The obvious one is the Snowy Mountain dam. But the problem is vast. There are 145 kilometres of interconnected tunnels, 80 kilometres of aqueducts, and 16 main dams. Besides providing hydropower for most of the east coast, it also irrigates the prime agricultural basin,' he explained. 'If they did succeed in setting off such a device, the disruption would be devastating to anybody in the area. And a national disaster on a biblical scale.'

Sergei spoke. 'From my experience, when the top guys go to the ground, bad things happen soon after.'

Chaz nodded. 'I agree. Enough waiting around. We will watch for a few days if we don't get any news from Vince and the boys. I say we give these guys a visit.'

# 61

While they kept Chen under observation, the same was happening back at their home base. Li Yang was watching the comings and goings of the rest of the "Umbrella Men".

When she discovered where they were staying, she called the number she had been given. She reported that Chen had not disclosed anything. They suggested she try and find who these new players were.

She had been watching the mansion for a couple of days, observing from inside a lookout van marked as a traffic statistics vehicle, again provided by the influential people directing her. So far, she had seen the daughter of the dead cop. She had seen her disguised as a jogger. Following her, she observed her doing stretches in front of another large house, and later another guy from the place who kept watch from a distance in an unmarked car. Li was sure they were trying to discover something about the occupants. She again reached out and was informed it was the house of the Assistant Prime Minister.

This got their interest, and they asked her to watch there instead.

# 62

Aurora returned to the house from her last run and informed the others.

'His car picked him up just as I was passing. This is the day he stays in his apartment in the city. He holds meeting all day according to his online calendar. Whenever he does this, he stays in his apartment in the city. David and Alan were able to find this out. Alan is there right now. I saw him park as I ran back.'

'Think it is time I put my old skill to use again,' Bill added.

Although retired from his London mob days, he still liked to keep his hand in. It was decided that as soon as the guy left, Bill would, as he put it, 'Have a peek inside.'

'Look for anything that could link him to Chen. I have a strong feeling this guy is knee-deep in this,' Vincent Savage QC said.

# 63

Aurora and Bill were parked a discreet distance from the house, and as soon as his official car picked him up, they sprang into action. Bill exited the car and walked to the house as if he owned it. At the front door, the locks opened in seconds as if he had keys. Entering, he closed the door.

Bill took only seconds to disarm the alarm. The first thing he did was check that the house was empty, then searched for his best escape route in case he was disturbed. He quickly located the office and went straight to the computer desk. Expecting the laptop to be password protected, he connected a piece of equipment he had brought specifically for this job and booted the laptop up. If the password was not larger than eight characters, he figured it would open while he checked the rest of the office.

He quickly discovered a safe behind a wall painting. It was hinged, and when he saw the safe, he mumbled, 'They must not expect the crooks in this country to be very smart.'

Seeing that it was an old model that he could open in his sleep, had it open within minutes and the contents spread on the desk. He took photos of everything while watching the progress of his device. When he finished photographing the documents, he carefully replaced them in the order he had retrieved them to avoid suspicion.

He searched the rest of the office but found nothing of interest. The ping of his device alerted him that the laptop was unlocked. He opened the laptop and inserted a USB stick to download the contents. The files were large, so it was going to take some time.

On the street, Aurora was keeping watch impatiently in the car. It seemed that Bill had been gone forever. So, when she saw a vehicle she didn't recognise drive up and turn into the driveway, she reacted. Dialling his number, she whispered, 'Somebody has driven up to the house.'

'Almost done, head home. I will take a more discreet route,' Bill replied, hanging up.

He received the signal that the download was completed. Checking quickly that everything was as he found it, he went to the alarm, reset it, and escaped from the rear.

Outside, the occupants of the car were getting out. Cyril got out of the passenger side, slamming the door in anger. When the driver emerged, Aurora gasped. She recognised her immediately. It was Christine Wolfe, the Police Commissioner.

'What is she doing here?' she mumbled. Although he was the minister in charge of police affairs, there was no reason she could see them to be meeting at his apartment.

Making a quick decision, she decided to see if she could find anything. When she got to the house, she crept along the side, hoping to see inside. Looking inside one of the windows, she could see Wolfe pleading and trying to hug him. She could not believe her eyes.

Then, just as she was about to turn and leave, her world went black.

# 64

Bill arrived back at the house, where an anxious crew greeted him. 'Everything went okay?' Vincent asked.

'No problems. The security he is using was a doddle. He will never know anybody has been there.' He tossed the USB to Alan to work on while he gave Vince his phone. 'I took photos of everything he had in his safe for you to check out.'

Vince's eyebrows arched. 'His safe?'

'Why not. it was as easy as opening a kid's money box,' Bill laughed as he poured himself a drink.

'Aurora tipped me off that somebody was coming. So, I waited for them to go in and disarm the alarm,' he explained. 'He came in with some female. They were arguing about something. He was angry with her coming to his office. But she was pleading with him that she had to talk to him about questions being asked about rumours of a terrorist attack. She said she would, and I quote, "Be unable to keep a lid on it much longer." The guy tried to console her. He said she was the Commissioner and to use her power. He told her this will be all over very soon, and that seemed to calm her down a bit. She asked him if he was sure. All I could make out was that everything would be resolved at a very public event. At that point, they started to move, so I decided to make myself scarce.'

It was David who responded first. 'Commissioner? That could only be Christine Wolfe. It sounds like we have discovered who is stalling the investigation. What on earth could be her motivation?'

'When I heard them talking, it was not like colleagues. It was more like a husband-and-wife argument.' Bill added.

'Well, perhaps that is the answer. The motive for any crime is usually down to two things, money or love,' Vincent added. 'Monica and Diego, could you guys investigate what big national events are coming up shortly? Something that could be televised and have the people's attention.' Both nodded, glad to be assisting. Vince continued, 'If you guys,' indicating David and Alan, 'can decipher anything from the material Bill had obtained. I believe that time is of the essence. This is coming to a head, and we still have no clear picture of who is pulling the strings. I believe it is time for my brothers to visit Chen.' Looking around, he suddenly noticed something wrong. 'Where is Aurora?'

Bill replied, 'She was outside when she alerted me to their arrival. She must be still keeping lookout.' Concern crossed his face. 'I better go and check on her.'

'We will go with you,' David said.

Alan and Vincent nodded, and they headed to where her car was parked. When they arrived at the minister's house, to their dismay, Aurora's car was still parked where they had left it. But no sign of Aurora.

They searched the area as quietly as they could so as not to raise suspicion. But there was no evidence of a struggle. It was as if she had vanished without a trace.

## 65

Cyril Stanford had managed to calm down Christine and convince her the go back to her duties. Before she left, he again had to convince her that Chen would not be a problem, and if any real threat appeared, he would inform her in plenty of time to act.

'Remember, we only use him because he is providing the assassin. So, the blame will fall firmly on his group's shoulders,' he lied.

She was unconvinced but reluctantly agreed, helped by his hugging her and reassuringly kissing her as he escorted her to the car.

Returning inside, he went directly to his office, where he took his encrypted phone and called Chen. It answered on the second ring. 'We have a problem. All this unwanted attention from whoever these new people are has made my contact on the inside very nervous. Are we still on target for our agreed date?'

Chen replied. 'My scientist has assured me that the device will be ready. It will be timed to detonate at the same time as my girl will be carrying out her assignment,' he said.

'Good. She will have to clean up the loose ends too. I am referring to the contact inside. We could be connected, you understand?'

Chen agreed. 'When you are ready, pass me the details, and I will arrange it. Together we will change the history of both of our countries.'

Cyril just grunted and hung up. 'Fucking fanatic,' he mumbled. If his arms specialist had not assured him that this crazy guy's device could not work, he would have been concerned by Chen's confidence.

He sat back in his chair and started to relax. Now that he was in the final stages of his plan, and with Christine soon to be out of his life, he could finally enjoy the position he believed he was destined for.

*Only a few days and I will be crowned Prime Minister. Everything is in motion. Nothing can disrupt the outcome now.*

# 66

Chaz crushed the phone in his hand as he received the new information from Vincent, shocked at the disappearance of his cousin. Vince assured him that they were doing everything to locate her. He then explained the discovery of the person's identity suppressing the investigation.

'Do you think she is the informant?' he asked.

'Hard to tell. It's more lightly somebody with access to inside information. But anything is possible. We will know more when the boys crack his computer files. They are encrypted. But Bill has put them in touch with one of his chaps who is a specialist in this stuff. Also, Diego and Monica believe they have uncovered a possible date for all this to go down. There is a big ceremony on the steps of Parliament House on Labour Day in Canberra. All the leaders of the parties and numerous officials will be in attendance. We think this is the intended date.'

'When is that?' Chaz asked.

'In five days. Have you discovered anything on your end?' Vince asked.

'Well, we know there is minimal security. Only Chen and three guys, plus some mystery woman. But she had disappeared.'

Vince replied. 'I believe that she may be the assassin. But right now, that's all we know.'

Chaz was silent for a moment. 'Okay, enough talk. Des is going to the tavern again tonight to pump the gardener for any additional information. Regardless, we are going to have a look inside. It is time we took the initiative.'

Vincent cautioned him to take care, knowing he was wasting his time. He could hear in his brother's voice as soon as he discovered that Aurora was missing. All hell was going to break loose.

# 67

Vladimir 'Vlad' Stalin knew that as soon as his usefulness ended, so was he. So, with this in mind, he came up with an idea to remove his problem. He had located Chen's hideout by back-tracing his calls to him. Now armed with information, he put his plan into action.

'I wish to speak to Bruno. Tell him I have information for him,' he told the guy that answered the number he had been given.

'Well?' replied the gruff voice of Bruno.

He explained that he had a lead on the location of Chen and his crew and said it was located somewhere in the Snowy Mountains, and he would have the exact location very soon.

Bruno sounded pleased. 'I will get my guys together. We will be ready, don't let me down,' hanging up without waiting for a reply.

'*Mudak*. Arsehole,' Vlad mumbled as he placed his next call. Chen answered. 'I have news. The Russians say that they are close to locating where you are. They will inform me when they find out. Be prepared because they will come in hard.'

'We will be ready. Let me know when they are coming. You will be rewarded. Check your account later.' He hung up.

Vlad smiled to himself. Perhaps he not only could he get out of this alive, but also a lot richer.

# 68

Des had managed to catch up with his gardener pal and, after pumping him with drink, was able to extract some valuable information.

'Something is going down for sure,' he said to Chaz and Sergei. 'He says all the staff have been given a week off. There is only one person retained for cooking. She arrives in the mornings, prepares meals for the day, and then leaves. She says that she has only caught glimpses of the Chinese. They are working on something in the basement. When I asked him what was down there, he said nobody was allowed there.'

Chaz gave him a hearty slap on the back. 'Great work. It would seem that the date is correct. They must be working on whatever they plan to use.'

'But how do they plan to transport it to the target?' Des asked.

'No idea. But whatever they are planning, we aim to disrupt before it happens.'

Sergei stepped in. 'How do we get in?'

'The plan is to try to gain entry without being noticed. If these guys are occupied in the basement, it should give us an opportunity. Sergei, I want you to keep watch in case they try to make a break for it. There is only the front entrance they can use. So, block that until we give you the signal. I will text you.'

The following morning, they were ready for the assault. They decided to wait until the cook who prepared the meals had left. Then they planned to make their entry. Parking in sight of the gate as soon as she drove out, Chaz and Des jumped out.

'Stay alert and wait for my signal. Remember, we have no idea what these guys are planning,' as they darted into the shrubs that surrounded the house.

When they got to the side of the house, they circled to the rear. Des was checking the windows as they slipped past. 'No sign of anybody,' he whispered.

They got to a door at the back of the house. Chaz tried the handle, finding it locked. Taking a slim knife out, he quickly jimmied the lock. Entering quietly, they began to explore. They had entered the kitchen where the food lay prepared on the table. To their surprise, there was no sign of activity continuing from room to room.

'Could they have left already?' Des asked.

Chaz shook his head. 'Let's check out this basement.'

They found the door at the end of the corridor. Trying the handle, to Chaz's surprise, it was unlocked. There were lights below the stairs, and they went down into a complete workshop crammed with all types of equipment, the use of which they had no idea.

'Check this out,' Des said, pointing to a large bench.

It was empty now, but something had been assembled there, judging by the equipment surrounding it. Examining it, Chaz replied in a worried voice, 'I don't know much about this stuff, but whoever was working here sure looks like they knew what they were doing.'

A thump from Des got his attention. He was pointing at the back wall to a heavy steel door. Again, to their surprise, it was unlocked. It swung open silently on its hinges despite its size. In front was a tunnel extending into the distance. It was well constructed and appeared to have been there for some time. It was illuminated by evenly spaced lamps mounted on the ceiling.

'Look at this,' Des said, pointing to some writing on the wall. 'Snowy Mountain Hydro,' he read. 'This has to be one of the service tunnels. I read there are hundreds of them. They started construction on this thing in 1949 and finished in 1972. Nobody knows where they all lead.'

'Well, it looks like these guys are serious. They must have bought this place some time ago to access this tunnel,' Chaz added.

'Why?' Des asked.

'Because this is their target. They intend to blow up the whole hydro scheme, and whatever they were constructing is down there somewhere. And we have to stop it!'

They continued for what seemed miles, descending deeper as they went. Finally, they entered a large chamber with a large door at the other end. Chaz gripped the handle and tested it to see if it would open.

At the moment it swung inward, they were greeted by the sight of Chen holding an Uzi.

'Welcome, gentlemen, we have been expecting you.'

# 69

Vlad decided that it was time to put his plan into action. He rang Boris to give him the story he had concocted.

'I will have the location today. Where are you? I will bring it to you,' he said.

'Just give it to me now,' Boris growled.

'I am collecting it later today. My source wants cash. I have to meet him in Thredbo,' he replied.

There was silence, then, 'We're in Thredbo. I will text you the name of the hotel. Call me when you are on your way,' hanging up.

Vlad smiled as he picked up the encrypted phone to contact Chen. He answered. 'I have news. My Russian contact tells me Boris Semenov expects to have your location later tonight. I suggest you take precautions.'

'Who is this Boris, and what is his argument with me?'

'His name is Boris Semenov, the leader of the Russian mafia in this country. He got word of your arrangement with Yakov, and after a little persuasion, he told him about your nuclear device.'

Chen was shocked into silence. Finally, he responded. 'Nonsense. There is no device.'

'It's not me you have to convince. He believes that if you were to commit such an act, it could do serious damage to his business. So, my advice is to prepare for a visit. The best I can do is tell you when they are coming.'

Chen took a deep breath. 'Make sure you do. The usual deposit will be in your account in moments,' and hung up

Vlad sat back and relaxed. All the pieces were now in place. Everything was proceeding like clockwork.

# 70

In her loft in Melbourne, Li Yang's encrypted satellite phone was answered on the first ring.

'I have important information. What I believe you have been waiting for.'

'Please hold,' the fellow asserted.

Soon a new voice came on the phone. He sounded distinguished. But as he spoke, she detected a note of sadness. 'Hello, Li.' He was one of the few that knew her real name.

'I have news for you,' she replied. 'The date has been confirmed for my assignment. Labour Day, at the location discussed. Also, I believe by his behaviour that Chen Wah Yim intends to detonate the device simultaneously. Do you think he may have a functioning device?'

There was silence before he replied. 'Nothing is certain at this time. Continue with your assignment. Anything else?'

'Only, judging from listening to Chen, he believes that the group calling themselves "The Umbrella Men" will try and stop them.'

'Do you think they might succeed?'

'I believe they are dead men. This means you have less than thirty-six hours,' she replied.

He paused for a moment before responding. 'I have no choice. I am dispatching some people to take care of this problem,' he replied.

'Something else. The client was seen leaving his house in the company of a woman. My source has revealed her identity. She is the Police

Commissioner. I believe we have the informant. What do you want me to do?'

'Proceed as planned. I will leave you to deal with this woman. What about the policeman's daughter?' he asked.

'Taken care of,' she replied, cutting the connection.

## 71

Chaz blinked to clear his vision as he regained consciousness. Chen greeting them was the last thing he remembered, then he felt a prick on his neck, and the next thing he knew was recovering consciousness.

He and Des had their wrists and ankles tied with plastic tape and were seated with their backs against the wall. Des still had his chin slumped on his chest, breathing gently. Chen and his cronies were hunched over a suitcase-shaped object on a large table in the centre of the chamber. Chen looked up to see Chaz had awoken.

'Welcome again, Umbrella Men. Glad you could join us. We watched with great interest as you searched my home,' indicting the array of TV screens with views of every room in the house. 'Sorry we could not greet you, but as you can see, we are swamped putting the final touches to our little surprise,' pointing to the device on the table.

At that moment, Des began to recover. 'What happened?' he asked.

'We got drugged, I imagine,' Chaz replied, nodding in the direction of Chen

'Correct,' Chen replied. 'So much more civilised than burning people in their car,' he replied sarcastically.

'Do you intend to explode that thing? We were led to believe that it would be impossible,' Chaz asked.

'I would have agreed with you a few months ago, but thanks to my learned friend, Cui Guozhi, and his contacts in North Korea,' indicating one of the guys hunched over the device, 'it is now operational. In any case, you will be able to bear witness to it in all its glory as you keep it company. Sadly, you won't be able to describe it to anybody as you will be vaporised.'

'And when is all this to happen?' Des asked.

He glanced at this watch.' In six hours and thirty-five minutes, at which time the second phase will be taken place.'

'Second phase?' Des asked.

He thought for a moment before replying. 'Well, I suppose there is no harm in revealing the details, considering your predicament. At the same time, Sun Yee On will send your Prime Minister to join you in the afterlife.'

'Is that the one who killed the policeman?' Des asked.

'No, we had nothing to do with that debacle. You will have to look closer to home for the culprit.'

'What about our cousin?' Des demanded. Chen looked confused, and Des realised that he did not know what he was talking about. 'The policeman's daughter. She is our cousin.'

Chen nodded, realising the connection. 'So, this is a family affair, which explains a lot. But sadly, I am afraid she has already met Sun Yee On.'

At that moment, Guozi called out to Chen. 'It is ready to be armed.'

He turned to the brothers. 'Would you like to see our handiwork?' he asked. Without waiting for a reply, he spoke to one of the guys. 'Dai cut them loose and shoot them if they try anything. Gentlemen, this is Dai Huang. He has decided to remain here and be part of today's history. So be assured he will kill you if you try anything.'

After they were released, they were escorted to the table where the deadly device sat.

'Would you like it explained to you?' he asked.

Turning to Cui, he indicated for him to explain, who began by pointing to a circular orb in the centre of the device. 'This is the core. It contains the fissional material encased in this metal casing to direct the explosion's force,' pointing to the C4 plastic explosives that surrounded it. 'Once Master Chen activates the timer, it is impossible to defuse. Any attempt will only result in instant detonation.'

Des was looking closely at the orb. 'You seem very interested,' Chen commented.

'Well, if this is going to kill us, I would like to know how it works. What are those plates that make up the casing?' he asked, pointing to the core.

Chen nodded to Guozhi to answer. 'For the nuclear explosion to occur, all the pressure created by the primary explosion must be equally distributed around the circumference. Those plates are designed to distribute the force directly to the core,' as he demonstrated an explosion by waving his arms in a wide arch.

Chen's phone chimed. He answered, listening without speaking. Hanging up, he turned to his comrades. 'Our other guests have arrived. Are you prepared?'

Dai Huang and the other one, Ding Fan, turned to address him. 'We are ready,' pointing to some stuff in the corner.

'I will make sure that your names are remembered in the new China you are helping to create.'

They bowed stiffly and then made their way over to prepare for whatever they had planned.

# 72

Outside the estate, Boris and his crew arrived, unaware that Sergei was observing them. Vlad directed them to the house, but when they made their entrance, he remained outside. Sergei watched as Vlad got into one of the cars and drove away.

Inside, Boris directed his men to search the place as he scanned the room for booby traps. But the site looked remarkably ordinary. He began searching for anything confirming that Chen had ever been here. He was now cursing under his breath for having trusted that rat, Vlad. He may have thought he had avoided his wrath. But he had arranged a surprise for him already.

He found some documents on one of the desks that he could not understand as they were in Chinese, but he at least confirmed he was in the right place. His men returned to tell him the place was deserted, but whoever was there had just left as there was still food prepared in the kitchen.

'There must be another exit. Search again,' he ordered.

# 73

Down below, Chen watched Boris and his men search the rooms on the screens.

'As you probably have realised, some others have discovered my location. But before you start holding out any hope of rescue, you can watch it all unfold on TV,' he said, pointing to the screens. 'I must depart now as my helicopter is waiting to take Cui Guozhi and me to a safe distance. But don't worry. We will watch the events unfold on national TV. It should be quite a show. Oh, one more thing. In case you had the idea of separating the orb from the explosive, I am sure you can guess, boom! Enjoy your last five hours and some minutes,' he said, consulting his watch, 'sealed behind the blast doors,' indicating the door they had entered by, 'and this one, which is equally as strong,' pointing to a smaller door recessed in the back wall.

Just at that moment, Guozhi indicated to the screens. Boris's men had assembled at the door, and it looked as if they were about to burst in. Chen looked at the remaining two, who by now had prepared themselves. Without a word, they bowed again and made their way to the main door. They were about to exit when Guozhi again brought their attention to the TV. A second group was approaching from the rear. They looked completely different in their behaviour. To Chaz, they were trained professionals by how they approached their tasks.

It was Cui Guozhi who spoke. 'Leave and complete the mission. I will remain and take care of this,' he said to Chen, who paused only for a moment, then gave a stiff bow and turned to exit. At the same time, the other three departed.

Chaz and Des heard the bolts and locks slam into position, sealing them inside. They turned their attention to the monitors to watch what was unfolding.

'Look,' Des said, pointing at one of the screens. They saw the two Chinese walking along the tunnel back to the cellar.

'What can they hope to do against those guys?' he asked.

'Nothing, I hope,' replied Chaz. 'Those guys are our best hope of getting out of here.'

Just then, Des pointed again. 'The other crew has arrived. Whose side do you think they are on?'

'Let's hope the Russians. The enemy of my enemy is my friend. And in this case, anybody that opens this door is my friend,' Chaz grunted.

## 74

Boris's men didn't take long to discover the entrance to the cellar.

They were just about to open it when they heard footsteps on the stairs. Standing back with guns raised, they watched as the door swung open. Standing there were the two Chinese guys with hands raised.

Dai Huang spoke in broken English, 'Take us to your boss, please,' as they both bowed stiffly.

The Russians were taken aback by their behaviour. The group leader indicated with his gun for the two Chinese to enter and make their way to the living area. As soon as Boris saw them, he realised neither of these guys was Chen.

'Where did you find these guys?' he asked.

The group leader explained what had happened. 'They asked to be taken to you.'

Boris turned to the Chinese, who were standing there quite calmly. 'Where is Chen?'

Huang just shrugged. 'Search the cellar,' Boris ordered his men.

'I would not advise that,' Huang responded.

Boris turned, 'Why, what is down there?' he snarled.

Dai Huang smiled, then replied, 'Destiny.'

Before Boris could respond, the group that had entered from the rear burst in. Both groups faced off with the two Chinese guys standing between them. One of the new groups began speaking in what Boris supposed was their language. He seemed to be demanding something. He was curious whether he was talking to him or the two Chinese.

His own guys were now waving their guns and demanding the others drop theirs. While at the same time, the leader of the other group was pointing his gun at the head of Di Huang, screaming at him to respond to his demands.

Instead of speaking, they both turned towards the leader and opened their jackets. He froze, dropping his gun. Boris could see the naked fear on his face as he screamed a Japanese word he knew very well, 'Kamikaze!'

At that moment, Boris knew he had made a fatal error as the two Chinese detonated their suicide vests.

# 75

## CANBERRA,
## AUSTRALIAN CAPITAL TERRITORY

Li Yang arrived at Canberra airport that morning and went directly to the building she had sourced previously. It was a partly completed office building about a mile from where her intended target was to be in approximately two hours.

She placed the carry case on a table she had set up prior to arrival, then went to the window to watch the proceedings for the Labour Day ceremony. It was to be attended by politicians and dignitaries from all parties in a display of solidarity. She had a clear sight of the preparations on the steps of Parliament House, and she smiled at the ease of finding a view like this within easy reach of her target.

Opening the case, she removed the disassembled parts of the SAKO TGR 71 sniper rifle. After assembling it, she placed it on the table and positioned the barrel on a small sack of sand she had readied. Lying prone on the table, she sighted the telescope, focusing on the flags fluttering in the spring breeze and making minor adjustments. When satisfied that the wind would not be a factor, she transferred her focus to the dais where the speeches would be delivered. Putting the crosshairs on the microphone, she breathed out and then calmed herself as she gently applied pressure to the hair trigger. The soft click of the hammer fell on the empty chamber. She softly murmured, 'Bang!' then insert a live 300-grain round into the magazine.

She relaxed and watched the large crowd assembling on this beautiful spring day on this public holiday. She watched the officials busy preparing the area for the dignitary's arrival. She glanced at her watch and saw it was just over an hour and a half until the agreed hour.

At the same time, she wondered what was taking place back at Chen's estate.

# 76

Chaz and Des jumped back in shock as the TV screens went blank and the explosion blast shook the room, filling the place with dust.

'What happened?' Des coughed in the dust.

'They were wearing suicide vests. They blew themselves up,' Chaz snarled. 'Burying us here!'

Des coughed again and went to inspect the device. 'This thing goes off in an hour and a half. We must try something,' he said.

Chaz had checked every corner of the room, trying to see if there was any way of opening the doors.

'I am open to suggestions because these doors are blast-proof and are locked from the outside.'

Suddenly, Des yelped and pointed across the room, 'Grab me that knife!'

Chaz saw a knife lying on the floor, one of many things scattered around the room the Chinese had left behind. 'Why?' he asked.

'Come here. I have an idea,' Des replied, indicating for him to come over. 'Give me the knife. Look here,' pointing to the sphere. 'See these metal panels? If I am right and we can remove one of them, it should interrupt the direct pressure he was saying it will need to create the nuclear explosion.'

As he carefully prised the gap around one of the pieces of metal, Chaz shrugged. 'Suppose we are going to go out with a bang. It might as well be with one of your plans.'

Des kept at it for another hour without much progress. Finally, he flung the knife down in frustration. 'I have barely made a dent in it,' he yelled in disgust.

'Why are you being so gentle?'

Des looked a Chaz in confusion. 'Well, if we are going to blow up anyway, why don't you use this?' Chaz said, handing Des a hammer, something else the Chinese had left behind.

Des looked at his brother for a second, then glanced at the hammer in trepidation. 'Toss you for it!'

Chaz just looked at him. Des shrugged. 'Just don't want to be blamed if we're killed!' Then he grabbed the hammer, picked up the knife and turned to the orb. 'Here goes nothing,' as he pushed the knife into the minor groove he had made in the plate. He smacked it as hard as he could, closing his eyes simultaneously.

To their surprise, nothing went *bang!* except for the steel plate hitting the cement floor. They stood in shock.

'It worked!' Des cried, grabbing his brother and hugging him in delight. The sober look on Chaz's face brought him back to earth. 'We are still going to die,' he said.

Chaz nodded. 'Even if your idea works, we will never know. The primary explosion will destroy everything in this room, us included. Come on, we might as well take a weight off our feet.' He led his brother over to the door where Chen had escaped. 'Okay, we have thirty minutes, so tell me, where did you come up with his idea?'

Des was silent for a moment. 'I saw it in a movie. George Clooney and Nicole Kidman were in it. I don't remember the name, but that's how he prevented a nuclear bomb from going off in some city in America.' Chaz was silent for a moment, then burst out laughing. Des proceeded to laugh along with his brother. 'If Dad could hear us now, I am sure he would call us the greatest pair of gobshites for getting ourselves into this mess.'

Chaz sat straight up. 'Shut up!' he snapped.

'That's your last words? Shut up!' Des replied.

'No, be quiet. Do you hear that?'

Des was silent for a moment. Then he heard a scraping noise.

'It's coming from the door,' Chaz said as he jumped to his feet and rushed over, putting his ear to it. Suddenly he felt it shudder as it slowly began to open.

They were greeted by the blackened face of Sergei. 'You are alive!' he yelled, hugging both of them in his massive arms. 'I don't believe it. I was sure you were dead.'

'We thought we were. How did you find us?' Chaz asked.

Sergei explained that when the house exploded and was reduced to rubble, he thought there was no hope. 'I thought you were buried alive. Then I heard a helicopter in the distance begin to spool up, so I went to investigate. I saw Chen and one of his accomplices come out of a door recessed into a hillside about a kilometre from the house. They made their escape in the chopper. So, I decided to see where they had come from. Luckily, the lights must be on a separate circuit, and I could follow their footprints in the dust until I found this place. What is it?' he asked, looking around.

Chaz pointed to the device on the table. 'That's a nuclear device. No time to explain. It's due to explode in ten minutes. Des thinks he may have prevented it, but the primary explosion will kill us if we don't get outside that door.'

Des pointed out there was no need to rush. 'If my idea doesn't work, the door won't make any difference. So, let's step outside and wait to see if my genius works,' he suggested.

Once outside the door, they shut it firmly. 'This is a blast door. But it would be better if we moved up the tunnel just in case we get lucky,' Chaz advised as they went to the first bend. 'This will do. Only four minutes to go, guys,' he said as he gripped his brother's hand.

Precisely on time, the floor shook, and everything went black.

# 77

At the steps of Parliament House, the invitees were assembled in their respective positions, awaiting the arrival of the Prime Minister and his deputy. The crowds had swollen considerably in anticipation of their arrival.

From her perch, Li Yang had a perfect view of the proceedings as she awaited the arrival of her target. She had just received a call from her contact in China.

'How are you progressing?' the now familiar voice asked.

'Just awaiting the arrival of the target. It will happen at the agreed time. Any news from Chen's place?'

There was silence for a moment, then the voice replied with a slight tremble. 'It is in hand as we speak. You will know if we fail.' Then the line went dead.

Li shrugged. Such was her life. She knew it could end at any moment, especially in her line of work. So, worrying about being killed by a nuclear bomb had never entered her mind. As she prepared for the job at hand, Michael Parker walked out waving to the crowd in his familiar laid back style.

A massive roar from the crowd greeted him. 'Mick! Mick!' they chanted.

He was followed by the right Honourable Cyril Stanford, who was greeted by much less enthusiasm. Smiling broadly, he waved to the crowd regardless.

Li Yang watched calmly as the Prime Minister walked to the dais. Sighting her target and taking a final check of the wind, she glanced at her watch. It was time.

She placed the crosshairs on her target and breathed out, then gently press the trigger. She watched as his head exploded in a halo of blood and brains. Before anybody could react, she had dismantled the gun and was calmly descending the stairs of the deserted building.

By the time they had managed to clear the steps where the body had fallen, she was already in a cab heading for her flight back to Melbourne.

# 78

Chaz, Des, and Sergei stood as the vibrations of the blast shook the wall that surrounded them. The light quickly came back on as some backup system came online.

Des spoke first. 'It must have worked!' as he jumped with joy.

Sergei was not convinced. 'How do you know?'

Chaz replied. 'Well, if that were a nuclear explosion, we would not be having this conversation. This place and everything for a couple of miles would be vaporised.'

Sergei picked Des up like a toy and flung him in the air. 'From now on, you are my brother. I owe you my life,' he declared.

As the giant Russian placed him gently down, Chaz said, 'Not just your life, but who knows how many other lives he has saved today,' and he gave his brother a clap on the back. 'Now, better get out of this place. Show us how you got in, Sergei.'

Chaz and Des followed Sergei along a long tunnel until they arrived at the exit. As they stepped out into the sweet air of freedom, they could hear the sound of sirens approaching in the distance.

'Time to make ourselves scarce. The last thing we need is to be trying to explain what has happened here to the police,' said Chaz.

Passing the remains of Chen's house and the surrounding area, Sergei stopped suddenly as he came to where he had left the car. The explosion had flattened the car, crushed by falling rubble.

'We are screwed,' Des cried.

Sergei thumped him. 'Don't worry. I have it covered,' he assured them.

He led them to a small side road where two late-model Range Rovers were parked. One of them had been damaged by large pieces of falling debris from the explosion, but the other one had been protected from the blast by the first car and looked remarkably untouched.

'Who owns these?' Chaz asked.

'Some other gang arrived just after Boris went inside, so I don't think they will need them,' he replied.

On inspection of the undamaged vehicle, to their delight, the keys were still in the ignition. 'I guess they were planning a quick getaway,' Des added as they jumped in.

Sergei took the wheel. They had only gone a couple of kilometres before a stream of emergency vehicles with a police escort passed them at great speed going in the opposite direction. They visibly relaxed as the realisation of what they had just survived began to sink in.

'That's something you don't experience every day,' Des said with a straight face. That made them burst out in laughter.

As they drove, Chaz settled in for the six-to-seven-hour drive back to the rest of the crew in Melbourne, wondering if there was any news about their cousin, Aurora.

## 79

Chaz, Des and Sergei arrived that evening at the Suarez's mansion. Everyone greeted them with delight as they crowded around to welcome them back. Maria had Des in a bear hug that threatened to choke him while the rest demanded what had happened.

After they settled down, drinks and food were provided for the exhausted adventurers. Chaz proceeded to fill them in. When he finished, Sergei gave his version of what he had observed from outside Chen's estate.

'So, Chen got away?' Vincent asked.

Sergei nodded. 'I saw him, and another crew member get into a helicopter he had waiting. But I was more interested in seeing if I could help my brothers.'

'Good job he did, or we would be buried alive,' Des added.

'You are amazing. You saved the world,' Maria yelled as she again choked him with a bear hug.

Des was embarrassed, not used to getting so much praise. 'Don't know about saving the world,' he blustered.

Chaz stepped in. 'All I know is that if Des had not come up with his idea, Chen would be celebrating the success of his plan, plus the fact, we would be dead.' He gave his brother a thumbs up, which only helped heap more praise on him.

It was Monica that brought their attention to the news. 'Have you heard about the assassination?' she asked.

They looked blankly at her. 'We only stopped to top up with fuel and grab some drinks. What happened?' Chaz asked.

Instead of replying, she turned on the TV, which was humming with continuous bulletins of the Labour Day catastrophe. They sat in silence as they watched the reports of the assassination of the Deputy Prime Minister, Cyril Stanford. Visibly shaken, the Prime Minister was addressing the camera, assuring the public that they would bring the culprit to justice.

Finally, Chaz asked. 'Wow. Was he an expected target?'

Vincent replied, 'Since you have been away, the boys and me,' indicating David, Alan, and Bill, 'we have managed to decipher some of the files in Cyril's computer, and these strange events have many sides. It would seem that Cyril is, or I should say 'was', one of many connected to a radical faction of Fabianism.'

'Who?' Chaz asked.

He went on to explain that the Fabián Society was founded in England in 1814. Many leading writers had dedicated themselves to "educating" society about the benefits of teaching the working class the benefits of socialism mainly, as some would agree, as a method of controlling productivity. They were staunchly anti-colonialism. He stopped when he saw his brother's eyes glazing over with tiredness.

'We are still working on finding who is behind all this and, more to the point, who is trying to disrupt it,' he added.

It was Chaz that brought them back to the present by asking, 'Have you any news on Aurora?' The worried look on their faces told him that the information was not good.

Alan answered. 'Nothing yet. I have put in a missing person's report and asked my contacts to keep their ear on the ground. We have been checking all the hospitals and the morgues. Nothing yet, which is good news. If the mob had killed her, we would have found d the body by now,' which was of little comfort.

## 80

Li Yang walked out of Tullamarine airport after an uneventful trip back to Melbourne. With a smile she nodded to one of the numerous security personnel scanning passengers for anybody of suspicion. He nodded in return, dismissing her as she went on her way.

Arriving at her Docklands apartment, she closed the lift gate behind her and unlocked the security door to her loft. She entered, then secured it behind her, tutting to herself to find the lights burning and the TV on.

'I see you have been making yourself comfortable,' she said to her guest, hearing the sound of a chain being dragged across the floor.

'You bitch! You drugged me and chained me up here like an animal,' yelled Aurora as she charged at Li, but the chain attached to her ankle pulled her to a halt.

'Sorry about that, but things were coming to a head, and I had to take you out of play or you would have come to harm,' she replied calmly.

She went to the kitchen to get herself a drink. 'Coffee?' she offered. Aurora just snarled and pulled at her restrain futilely. 'Listen, if I intended to harm you, you would be dead already. I left you with food and water, and by now I am sure you have discovered this place is soundproof. So, I suggest you relax and I will explain everything to you,' she said as she continued to prepare the coffee.

Aurora pointed at the television. 'Was that you?'

Li did not reply. She just handed the coffee to her and said, 'Did you know that man was instrumental in your father's death?' Aurora's mouth dropped in shock. 'If you promise to behave, I will release you and try to make sense of this. Your father's death is just one part of a much bigger plot. So, do you want to discover who killed your father?'

Aurora sipped the coffee with shaken hands and nodded. Li bent down and uncoupled the shackle that secured her to the chain. 'Now you are probably thinking of trying got overpower me...'

Immediately Aurora grabbed her, only to find herself on her back. Not being deterred, she jumped to her feet again, sure that she should be able to overpower the more petite woman. She was mistaken. Evert time she grabbed Li, she slipped out of her clutches. After many futile attempts, Li put her in a chokehold and said, 'We can do this all day, or you can sit down and listen to what I have to say. Then if you are not satisfied, we can resume.'

She released Aurora, who got to her feet and begrudgingly sat down.

'Let's begin. Chen Wah Yim contacted me to take out an important political figure.'

'Cyril Stanford,' Aurora snapped, pointing at the TV.

'Hardly. He was the person that wanted my services. He wanted me to kill the Prime Minister. I told him that when I take a contract, I never fail. Either the target dies, or I do.'

'So, you lied to him,' Aurora said.

'Not at all. You see, he was not in a position to engage my services. Because he was already a dead man. When Chen first contacted me, I was not interested until I received a call from a very influential person in China. He told me what would be asked of me and asked if they could engage my services. This was a person you did not refuse.'

'What did he want?' Aurora asked.

'He asked that I assassinate the person that tries to hire me to kill the Minister. And that's what I did.'

## 81

Li went to the kitchen and returned with a bottle of schnapps and two shot glasses. 'Here, this will help,' pouring two glasses.

Li downed the drink. Aurora followed suit and choked for a moment. Seeing Li smile, she thrust out her glass for a refill. 'Not bad. I've had stronger,' as she downed a second one. 'So, who is this mysterious person, and why would he want to prevent the assassination of the Prime Minister?'

'That is something he will have to answer. This is not over yet. There is the matter of your father's killing to be resolved.'

Aurora held out her glass again. 'I believe, judging from what I have uncovered, he was killed because he discovered how the equipment was transported.'

Li shook her head. 'You are wrong. He was killed because he discovered the identity of the informant.'

'Do you know who it is?' she demanded.

Nodding, she replied, 'Yes, but I will have to talk to my people. I believe it is time we combined resources. What I propose is that you return to your "Umbrella Men"...'

Aurora cut her off. 'They are my cousins. They just invented that silly name to upset that Yakov prick.'

Li smiled again. 'I think it is a good name. So far, they have done a good job. Rescuing you from being killed, getting the Serbs to set themselves on fire. Also, without them, we would not have discovered where Chen planned to launch his attack.'

A worried look crossed Aurora's face. 'I hope they are all right. They went to try and stop whatever Chen was doing.'

Li avoided looking at her and instead replied, 'Well, whatever they did, one thing is for sure, there was no nuclear explosion.'

Aurora persisted. 'Why won't you tell me who killed my father?'

Awkwardly, Li tried to console her. 'What I can tell you is that the person responsible had more to answer for. But I can assure you justice will be done, and you will be present to witness it.'

Aurora dried her eyes, oddly comforted by this cold-blooded killer.

Li broke the silence. 'I will take you back to your friends. Have you any contacts in high places in the government or police?' she asked.

Aurora told her how Chief Inspector David George and her father's old partner, Alan Moffatt, were helping unofficially. The Savage brothers and their odd group of friends seemed to have contacts.

'Until I contact you, see if they can find a way to speak to the Prime Minister. But it has to be through unofficial channels. Believe me when I tell you his government is badly compromised.' Aurora began to question her, but Li cut her short. 'Let's go. I'm taking you home.'

Downstairs, Li wheeled her BMW S1000 RR out and pushed the starter button. The bike roaring it into life. 'Here, put this on,' handing her a helmet. Aurora took it and sat on the pillion seat. Li kicked the bike into gear. 'Hold on tight,' she said as they roared away.

The journey seemed to only take minutes when she pulled up to the entrance to the Suarez's mansion. Stepping off, Aurora turned to Li. 'How will I contact you?'

'Don't worry. I will be in touch,' she said, roaring away.

Aurora watched her vanish, leaving her with a strange glow.

## 82

When the butler opened the door to answer the strident ringing of the bell, he was pushed aside by Monica, who had rushed to see what was going on.

'Aurora!', she screamed, embracing her with all her strength. 'We were worried sick. What happened?'

Without waiting for a reply, she ushered her into the living room, where everybody was gathered. Aurora was delighted to see the brothers safe and sound as they explained what had happened at Chen's place. The excitement endured for some time as everybody clambered for news of her capture. Finally, calm was restored, and Aurora explained what had happened from when she had felt the hand encircling her face and the smell of chloroform to her regaining consciousness in a soundproof loft and finding herself chained. She had discovered that she had been provided with food and drink and had access to the television, where she heard about the assassination of Cyril Stanford. Then the arrival of her captor and what she had disclosed to her.

'Who is she?' Chaz asked. 'She never told me her name, but she did tell me she knows who killed my dad.'

'Yet she admitted to killing Stanford on the instructions of some mysterious person from China?' Vincent asked.

She nodded. 'I believe she is on our side. But she has to follow whatever this guy says. She asked if we could get some outside help to speak to the Prime Minister. But it has to be through back channels. She says that this is not over yet. There are, and I quote, "Other parties involved at the highest level of the government".'

Vincent stepped in. 'I believe we can fill in some of the gaps from what we have discovered on Cyril's laptop. As I said, Fabianism is still benignly followed worldwide with good results, depending on your point of view. But this group that Sanford was involved with had a very different and very radical view of how it should be implemented. These people were a driving force for the implementation of Brexit, and their success in Britain has emboldened them. During his time in England he had become deeply involved, so when they turned their attention to Australia, their followers reached out to him over here.'

'Who?' Chaz asked.

This was when Alan spoke. 'That's where it gets interesting. Their contact was Christine Wolfe, our Police Commissioner, and that's when it gets weird,' as he nodded for Vincent to continue.

'From what we can decipher, it was about how they could promote a return to the Australia of old. When the 'White Australia' policy existed. Nothing would have eventuated, I am sure, until two things happened. One, Cyril became involved with this Chinese terrorist group; and two, Christine fell madly in love with him. When he asked her to suppress the investigation, he told her his scheme of killing the Prime Minister was planned to coincide with the detonation of the dirty bomb. He believed that with him in the top job and the outrage at what had happened, he could reintroduce zero immigration and foreign investment. Effectively turn back the clock, and leaving him with free rein to promote their distorted ideas.'

'But now that he is dead, surely the problem is over?' Des interjected.

'Not at all,' Aurora replied. 'This is why the assassin girl wants you to open dialogue with Michel Parker. Remember, it was still a minister that was killed, and when they excavate Chen's house and find a small dead army under the rubble, plus the remains of the device, all hell will break loose. That's why he needs to know what's going on.'

'I don't understand why she or whoever pulls her strings would want to help. What is their angle?' Vincent asked.

'She told me she would try to convince this person to meet with us and combine forces. She assured me she would be in contact. And I believe her,' she replied with a determined voice.

Vince frowned, then decided to change the subject. 'So, do any of you have the Prime Minister's private number?' he asked, not expecting a reply.

But to his surprise, David replied. 'I don't have his number, but I know somebody that should be able to get it,' he said, then continued. 'When I was with the anti-terrorist squad, we worked closely with the CIA. I became friendly with this guy. Cliff Granger is his name, and we have helped each other from time to time. I can reach out to him,' he suggested.

'Great. Do that. But remember to tell him to keep it close to his chest. We don't know how far they have infiltrated the power base here. You can be sure that they will try to exploit this debacle,' Vincent added. 'In the meantime, Bill has been in contact with a pal of his in MI6 to see if we can discover who is behind this back in England. The chaps have always worked with the Old Bill when something that is not cosher comes to our attention,' he said with a grin on his face.

'Do we know who is directing this from there?' Chaz asked.

Vince shrugged. 'So far, we have discovered some initials they go by. They are called L G F in the files we have managed to decipher. We should have more news soon,' which prompted a nod from Alan.

'So, what next?' Des asked.

It was Chaz that replied. 'We go on the offensive. I take a poor view of anybody trying to blow up my brother and me with an atomic bomb.

That was just overkill. And I intend to sort them out. Sergei, can you locate this Vlad character and find out what he knows?'

Sergei nodded. 'I will ask him, and he will tell me everything,' he replied in a voice that made a few of them shiver.

Chaz continued. 'Now, what is Christine Wolfe's involvement in all this?'

# 83

Police Commissioner Christine Wolfe was seated in her office trying to come to terms with what had just happened. Hearing that her lover had been shot instead of the intended target left her in disbelief and denial. At first, she found herself in tears. Then, as her instincts for survival kicked in, she began exploring her exposure to this disaster.

She now cursed herself for allowing her passions to interfere with their mission. When their mentor and leader in London had reached out to her to contact Cyril and aid him with his outlandish scheme, she had questioned him about the risk. She had real doubts Cyril and this Chinese group could succeed. He had assured her that, regardless, the attempt would be sure to inflame the public, and she would be well placed to 'discover' the plot by a terrorist group who were behind the whole thing.

When she told him about the romantic entanglement, to her surprise, he encouraged it. 'Use it to our advantage,' was his advice.

The gloves now off, she began to enjoy it. Cyril was charming, and when she was with him, she actually believed he would succeed. She even foolishly began to fantasise as the wife of the new Prime Minister.

That dream was gone. Now her survival would depend on how the resulting chaos was handled. So far, all focus was on the hunt for the assassin. The only news about Chen's plan was a notice from her desk about a mysterious explosion that had destroyed a large estate in the Snowy Mountains. She knew it was Chen's place from Cyril's description of his visits there, and she thanked her lucky stars she had never taken him up on his offer to accompany him.

Reluctantly she retrieved her satellite phone and made a call to London. Lincoln George Foster MP picked up the call on the first ring. He had expected it since receiving the news of the botched assassination attempt and Cyril Stanford's demise.

'Hello Christine, how lovely to hear from you. So sorry for your loss,' he said in a voice that reeked of insincerity.

She did not react. Instead, she thanked him, and said, 'As you can imagine, it has been a terrible shock. I have no idea who did this unless Chen had something to do with it.'

'Tut, my dear, do you not remember what I told you when he came with his plot? I said to you that, regardless, we would capitalise on it. Now tell me what the response has been so far?'

'The anti-terrorist squad have taken charge of the investigation. I receive reports as my department oversees all departments. So far, all they have identified is where the shot was taken from. They say it was the work of a professional hitman.'

'Don't bother yourself with that. What of Chen's attempt? It must have failed, or it would be front page news.'

She told him about the explosion at his house. 'I assume that whatever he attempted must have destroyed his home instead.'

This brought a yelp of delight from Foster. 'Wonderful. When they excavate the site, the radiation readings will be off the charts. It will be uncovered that a Chinese terrorist group tried to detonate a nuclear device on Australian soil. When that happens, our efforts will be rewarded. Control of your country will be handed back to the nationalists. Borders will be closed, and trade barriers will return,' he assured her.

'How will they know about the Chinese?' she asked.

'You will help them. Time to take the glove off and do your job. If you succeed, a place in the government is assured. Keep me posted,' as he cut the call.

Walking back to her office, she began to relax a little. *He is right. I am the Police Commissioner. I can control this.*

# 84

Sergei had a fair idea of where Vlad would be. Back in the old days, the Russians used a converted warehouse as a hideout. It had not been used for some time, and any new guys would have no idea about it.

When he got there, the first thing he did was check the underground parking. There was only one car there, and by the condition, he could see it had not been there very long. He then headed for the upper loft where the safe house had been established. As soon as he got there, he could hear movement inside.

'Vlad, it is Sergei. You can open up. I am not here to kill you,' he assured him. There was silence for a moment, so Sergei continued. 'You had better talk to me because the next people that find you may not be as accommodating.'

With that, he heard the locks being opened, and the door opened slowly to reveal a very dishevelled Vlad standing there with one hand behind his back. 'If you are considering shooting me, that better be a cannon behind your back. Because no gunshot will stop me from tearing your head off,' Sergei said as he pushed him out of his way.

Vlad looked outside to see if he was alone, then locked the door again. 'How did you find me?' he asked as he followed Sergei into the loft.

From the smell, it was evident that Vlad had not left this place since returning from Chen's house. 'I watched you playing charades with Boris and saw you leave them to their fate, which I am sure you had a hand in. In case you don't know, the Chinese blew the place up, killing all inside, including some other military group that arrived just in time to get blown up with the rest of them. So, you can forget about lying to me because you can be sure that the Russians will soon discover your part in the death of their leader. If I can find you, how long do you think it will take them when they find out he is dead?'

Vlad stood there quivering, then walked to a makeshift kitchen, opened the refrigerator's freezer, and took out a bottle of Vodka. 'I need a drink,' he announced.

He poured himself a large glass and handed the bottle to Sergei. Then he sat and began to tell him how he found himself in this dilemma. After he finished his story, he slumped down in resignation at his untenable situation.

Sergei refilled his glass. 'Do you still have contact with Chen?' he asked.

Vlad shrugged. 'I don't know. All I have is a number. Why?'

Instead of answering, Sergei took the bottle of vodka and downed a large gulp. 'Stay here and wait for me to contact you. I may be able to help you.'

Vlad raised his head as a small glimmer of hope filled his stricken face. 'Why would you help?' he asked.

'Because the enemy of my enemy is my friend,' he said, leaving Vlad in his misery, nursing his vodka.

## 85

Sergei reported back to the Umbrella Men's headquarters, as they were now calling it.

'Great news, let's keep him on ice until we decide how to use him,' advised Chaz. 'Things are moving from this end. David has news also,' handing over to him.

'I've spoken to my guy in the CIA, and he will reach out. I told him of the urgency, and he assured me he would return to me within the day.'

'Great stuff,' Chaz replied. 'Bill had discovered their British kingpin's name. He is an MP called Lincoln George Foster, which accounts for the initials we found on the computer. He has a strong nationalist agenda and is a member of the Fabian Society. Which in itself is pretty harmless. But behind the scenes, Scotland Yard has been monitoring his connection to a radical underground sect of the organisation of which he is the reputed leader. But to date, they have not been able to get any concrete evidence.'

'What is it with these English, with three or four names?' retorted Des. 'Are there so many Lincolns that they have trouble being identified? Whatever happened to nicknames?' There was a burst of laughter, and Des could not contain himself. 'What is it with you and this woman? She kidnaps you and chains you up, and now she's your best friend?'

Aurora blushed. 'It's just a girl thing.'

Before Des could say anything else, a swift kick in the shins from Maria shut him up.

Vincent took up the conversation. 'Now we have to hope they don't uncover what happened at Chen's place before we have a chance to talk to the top man.'

As he was talking, Aurora hurried into the room, holding her phone. 'She is on the phone,' she said excitedly. 'The person she has been working for in China is flying in. She wants to set up a meeting.'

Vince took charge. 'Is she still on the line?' She nodded. 'Where does she want to meet?' he asked.

She spoke to whoever was on the phone, then told him, 'She suggested they come here.'

Vince looked around at the group to see the reaction. Chaz was the one that spoke. 'I trust Aurora's judgment. The way I see it, the more help we can get, the better. I say go for it.'

Without waiting. Aurora spoke to Li. 'Yes, they say come here. When do you expect him to arrive? What time is his flight?' She started to laugh. 'Of course, he has a private jet. Okay, we will expect you this evening,' and hung up.

Vince looked at his brothers, but they just shrugged. 'Looks like we should prepare for company,' Monica announced.

# 86

The doorbell rang shortly after eight o'clock in the evening. Aurora had received a call about half an hour previously to let her know they were on their way. The atmosphere was electric in the house in anticipation of meeting their mystery guests.

Aurora rushed to welcome them. The sight of Li Yang greeted her and an older Asian-looking man. The first impression was that he had an aura of dignity, but she also detected a great sadness.

Before she could give it more thought, Li spoke. 'Perhaps we should go inside. We don't want to be noticed, do we?'

'Of course, come in. Everybody is waiting inside.' Leading them into the living room, where they were gathered.

'Everybody, this is...' then she turned to Li, 'I don't know your name.'

'Apologies. I should have introduced myself. I am called many names, but for you, I will use my real name, Li Yang,' gazing at Aurora.

She then turned to her companion, but before she could introduce him, he raised his hand and began to speak. 'With your permission, before I introduce myself, I would like to explain what brings me and all of you to this point. First, I wish to say that I must take responsibility for what has happened. Life in my country has changed. Everything has politics involved in it. Anything that brings negative attention is considered a disgrace to the perpetrator and every family member. What has happened to this point has been caused by somebody trying to protect their family's reputation, which we call "Face", even perhaps their complete disappearance. None of what I say is to be viewed as an excuse but rather as how something like this has happened. And perhaps what can be done to rectify the damage. You see, my name is Chen Liang. I am a member of the Ruling Council. I am also the father of Chen Wah Yim, the person responsible for the attack on this country.'

There was silence for a moment then everybody began to speak at once. Vincent called for calm. 'Let the man speak. Remember, he has come to us. That couldn't have been easy for a man in his position. It would appear that whatever has brought us to this point, we all agreed that finding a way out of this disaster is in all our interests. Remember, there were other players involved besides Mr Chen,' nodding in the direction of the older man in a show of respect, for which he received a stiff bow.

Liang continued his story. 'My son's misguided doctrine to me seemed like a lot of young men in China trying to rebel against our restrictive lifestyle. That was until I received word of his outlandish scheme. But before I could react, I was informed about him being contacted by that corrupt politician who wanted to assassinate the Prime Minister. Fortunately, he asked my son to help him find an assassin. When I heard that they had reached out to Li, I contacted her before she committed to his task. That is when I asked her to take my assignment first.'

Chaz asked him. 'What did you ask Li?'

'To remove the person that asks her to kill the Prime Minister,' he said.

Alan and David reacted. 'Hold on. We are still police officers. Don't say anything that could incriminate yourself.'

'As a leader in our government, I asked a member of a special security squad to prevent an international incident. You see, Li Yang is, or I should say was, the top agent in that unit. Her task for our government was to pose as an assassin for hire. That way, we could influence the outcomes depending on the benefit to the Communist Party.'

'So, in effect, you became judge and jury. Depending on who the target was?' David asked.

'We felt it was a little more subtle than the methods employed by the Americans,' he replied.

'Enough,' Vincent said sharply. 'This is not some international court. Remember what we are here for, to stop some warped nutcase in England bring down a democratically elected government. So, stay on track.'

Guang turned his attention to Vincent. 'Can I take it you are the leader of the "Umbrella Men"?' he asked. This brought a murmur of laughter from the room.

'That title is reserved for my crazy brothers,' Vince replied.

Guang spoke. 'It would seem, in both cases, it is family matters that have brought us here. In my case, sadly, the responsibility for all of this falls on mine.'

To everybody's surprise, it was Diego that responded. 'Señor Guang, I, we,' indicating his wife, Monica, 'we must also shoulder some of the blame. These boys would never have been dragged into this without the mess we created.'

This prompted an outcry from the family. Alan agreed with the sentiment, adding, 'If not for your actions causing them to be involved, they would not have been able to save Aurora's life,' to nods of approval.

Guang now said, 'They also averted a world-changing event. If anything, you should be thanked.' He turned to Li. 'Li. I have not had time to speak to you, but sadly the people that died in the explosion were members of your unit. Perhaps it is time for you to tell your perspective of what has happened.'

## 87

Li Yang nodded. 'That is or was our job. I have not been connected directly with my unit for many years since I took this role. As far as my country is concerned, I don't exist. But as Vincent has pointed out, this is a conversation for another time. As Guang has said, being able to follow the brothers to Chen's hideout, perhaps we would not have found it in time. He was cautious not to divulge anything of my presence. I was only there to kill the Prime Minister except when something strange happened. Cyril reached out to him for help. His informant was panicking because some policeman had discovered her involvement and wanted to speak privately before reporting it.' She directed her attention to Aurora. 'I had intended to tell you this personally, but we were short on time. The policeman was Aurora's father. They wanted me to kill him.'

This brought a gasp from Aurora, who made to speak.

'Let me finish. I contacted Guang, and he advised me to act as I would normally, which I did. When I took a contract, I had the freedom to "rescue the target". In other words, advise them that it was in their interest to vanish.'

It was Chaz that asked. 'And if they refused?'

'I told them that was their choice. Vanish, or I do what it was paid to do. They always vanished. So, I went to where the policeman had arranged to meet the informant. I intended to observe who was present and warn him of the threat to his life.' She paused. 'That's when things went wrong. The informant arrived on foot and sat in the passenger seat. At first, the conversation seemed somewhat normal, then suddenly the spy turned and attacked him, stabbing him in the neck. I could see instantly that it was fatal. He lost consciousness almost immediately. He had no time to react. It would have been very swift,' again directing her attention to the stricken Aurora.

'Did you not suspect that they might try something like that?' Chaz asked.

'No, remember I was supposed to be there to kill him. Why would they do it themselves?'

'So, what happened?' he asked.

'She jumped out of the car in a panic, ran to where her car was parked and vanished.'

'She?' he asked.

'Yes, it was a woman, the same woman I saw in the car with Cyril the day I picked up Aurora. It was the Police Commissioner, Christine Wolfe. She killed your father with a fountain pen. It had to be a panicked attack, and she hit a vital spot by chance. Sadly, one in a million.'

'So, did you set the car on fire?' Chaz asked.

She shook her head. 'I reported to Chen what had happened, and he said for me to leave it and he would get somebody else to take the fall.'

'Yakov Milosevic,' Sergei added. 'He screwed that one up. You will be glad to hear that it didn't end well for him.' When they all stared at him, he grinned. 'No, it was not me, but whoever did the deed burnt him in his car at the same place as James McCormac was burnt.

Li sat without an expression on her face as she could feel Aurora's gaze on her. At that moment, David's phone began to ring. He jumped up and stepped outside, then returned a few minutes later to announce, 'It's on. We are meeting the Prime Minister in Kirribilli House tomorrow.'

## 88

**KIRRIBILLI HOUSE**
**SYDNEY, NSW**

Chaz, Des, and the two police officers, David George and Alan Moffatt, flew to Sydney the following morning and arrived at the Prime Minister's house on Sydney Harbour around lunchtime. The PM's assistant ushered them into a large meeting room and asked them to make themselves comfortable. The Prime Minister would be with them after his conference call with the President of the USA.

The night before, Vincent advised that the version of the event disclosed to the Prime Minister should not put him in a compromising position. With that in mind, the brothers were to relate a sanitised version of events when they disclosed what they had discovered.

Five minutes after arriving, the Prime Minister burst into the room with incredible energy. 'Sorry for keeping you waiting. I was on a call with Craig,' referring to the current president of the United States of America, Craig Hillgrove.

'In fact, one of his countrymen has reached out to arrange this meeting. Which of your gents is 'Rambo'?'

David raised his hand. 'That would be me, sir.'

'Enough of the 'Sir', call me Mick. Now, what is so essential is that I have to speak to you at this difficult time?'

David replied. 'It is for that very matter that we had to speak to you with this urgency. We have uncovered who is behind both events and hope that with your approval, we can resolve this without creating an international incident.'

'Yes, I was only informed of the dirty bomb this morning,' he said, shaking his head. Then he looked at Chaz and Des. 'Am I to take it that you disarmed the nuclear device? Are you scientists?' he asked.

'No. I just...' Des started to say before he disclosed that it was something he had seen in a Hollywood movie.

Chaz stepped in. 'My brother has always had an interest in science. He reads everything he can get his hands on. Which thankfully came in handy. Thank goodness it worked,' he said, hoping to deflect the line of questioning. 'What is most important is ensuring that the site is not excavated and the bodies discovered before we have contained what has happened. It would be sure to draw the unwanted attention of the press and play into Cyril Stanford's plans.'

'What has this to do with Cyril? Is it connected to his assassination?' the PM asked.

'I believe we can answer that,' David replied.

He disclosed Cyril's involvement in the death of James McCormack and his plan to assassinate the Prime Minister and take the job for himself. He had hatched the scheme to combine it with Chen's plot.

The PM was thoughtful. 'I will have to alert the authorities. They are searching for the assassin as we speak.'

'That would be unwise. We have discovered there are others involved in the plot at the highest levels of government. We have no idea whom to trust,' Alan interjected. 'There is more,' and he disclosed Christine Wolfe's involvement as Sanford's lover and mole. 'Plus, her being the one that killed James McCormack.'

Michael Parker sat down as he tried to digest these revelations. 'You're telling me that the Deputy Prime Minister and the Police Commissioner conspired with some terrorist group the destroy the Snowy Mountain scheme and kill me? All because they wanted to take my job?' he asked.

'They are not working alone. A radical group in England leads them. They are part of a splinter group. A spin-off of the Fabian Society led by a maverick MP, Lincoln George Foster,' Alan added.

'If this gets out, true or not, the backlash could devastate our economy and international relations for years. I don't know about you fellows, but I need a drink,' as he called his assistant to provide something more substantial than the tea and coffee provided.

When they had drinks, Chaz put forward the plan they had conceived.

'You want me to offer that bitch a promotion?' the PM asked, nearly choking on his whiskey at their suggestion. 'Why would I do that?'

'Keep your friends close and your enemies closer,' Chaz said. 'If this works out, she will never take up the post.'

'How can you be so sure?' Mick Parker asked.

Des was the one that replied. 'It is better, considering your position, you don't know all the details. What you don't know can't hurt you. Slainte!' he said, raising his glass.

# 89

Christine Wolfe was sitting in her office poring over all the activity in the search for whoever was behind the assassination of her former lover. Something she would like to know as she figured she could very well be next on the list. She was also surprised that nothing had emerged about the explosion at Chen's compound. All she had heard was that some sort of gas pocket could have been responsible. She could do nothing to influence the excavation without drawing attention to herself, so she wondered what her next move should be.

As she picked up her favourite Dupont fountain pen, she suddenly remembered its terrible history, dropping it with a shudder. When James McCormack had requested a private meeting, she knew at once that he had discovered something about her involvement in suppressing his investigation. Contacting Cyril, he assured her he would take care of it. She now cursed herself for disregarding his advice. She had decided to meet with McCormack with the hope that she was mistaken. But when he confronted her with evidence, she lost control and attacked him with the pen she always carried with her. When she saw that he was dead from her attack, she panicked and ran. She then called Cyril to cover her mess, which resulted in the gruesome burning of his body.

Her phone ringing broke her train of thought. Her secretary told her that the Prime Minister was on the line and wished to speak to her. She started to perspire, and her hand shook, wondering if she had been discovered. Taking a deep breath, she told him to put the call through.

'Good morning, Christine. I hope you are holding up in these difficult times. I am calling you with some good news. I have just received word that one of the people investigating the dreadful assassination of our good friend, Cyril Stanford, has a promising lead as to the culprit.'

She gulped silently. 'That's great news. I am surprised it has not come to my attention.'

'There is a reason. This officer has been working undercover and came across the information by chance. It is for that reason that I have contacted you. Due to Cyril's untimely death, we need someone to replace him in his position of Minister of Defence. So I have decided to promote you to the position. It is high time you joined the government. Welcome aboard.'

She could not believe her ears. *Finally, I'm getting the recognition I deserve.* 'I don't know what to say. I am honoured.'

He continued. 'Now, to matters at hand, I have formed a special task force to bring the people that perpetrated this dastardly act to justice. I have placed the chap that uncovered the lead to head it up. His name is Chief Inspector David George from South Australia, and his assistant, Detective Sergeant Alan Moffatt. Please give them any assistance you can. They are to report directly to me. And again, congratulations,' as he ended the call.

She immediately searched online to investigate this David George. She already knew who Alan Moffatt was. He was the former partner of James McCormack, and she knew he was not involved in his investigation into her. Scrolling through the search pages, she learned that Chief Inspector David George had a formidable history in the police force, receiving many commendations. He had been on the Major Crimes squad and was recently involved in national security with the anti-terrorism unit. From what she could discover, he was just another honest cop.

She decided to give him a call. A few minutes later, she was talking to him. 'Christine Wolfe here. I am just calling you to congratulate you on your promotion,' she said in her cheeriest voice.

'Thank you, Commissioner, or I should say, Minister. The Prime Minister told me of his plan to bring you into the fold,' he replied.

'Well, it has not been announced, so let's keep that to ourselves. I hear you may have a lead as to the assassin?' she inquired.

'Yes, I can't go into detail. But my investigation discovered a link to a radical Chinese cell. I will keep you posted. But now, the PM wants to keep it between us.'

'Agreed, keep me in the loop. I will make sure that your investigation is kept under the radar.'

Goodbyes were said as she hung up. As she rolled her Dupont pen in her fingers, a feeling of some relief came over her.

*I am back in control. I will miss you, Cyril, but a girl has to look out for herself in this cutthroat world.*

# 90

Chief Inspector David George hung up the phone. 'She's in. It looks as if Michael Parker convinced her to play along. She has assured me she will keep a cap on other investigations.'

'True to form. Anything to save her neck,' Chaz replied.

Chaz, Des, David, and Alan had returned to Melbourne that evening. They were back at their headquarters in the Suarez mansion, satisfied they had convinced Mick Parker to trust David and Alan to keep his government shielded from any negative fallout. This gave them a bit more flexibility in their plans. When Vincent outlined his plan, they thought he was going too far, but when he pointed out what those people had attempted to do and were still forging ahead with their plans, they agreed that it was time to stretch the rules a little.

'Have you managed to do anything about controlling the excavation of the bomb site?' he asked David.

He nodded. 'We were just in time. The local CFS was called in first and lacked the equipment to excavate the place. So they contacted the local government for assistance. I spoke to the local fire chief and informed him that the scientists from The Snowy Mountain scheme suspected a pocket of natural gas was the probable culprit and to create a no-go area around the site until the relevant authorities could assess what action to take. I have our crew on the way to ensure that nobody goes near the place.'

'Perfect, we can prevent anyone from discovering what happened there,' Vincent replied.

'What about Chen? He and that bunch of fanatics will want the public to know what happened, failure of the device or not. Anyway, where is he?' Bill asked.

'Chen is with Li Yang at the Chinese Embassy. That's where he ran to after he set the device. It would be unwise to let the Prime Minister know of his existence at this stage. Also, there's no way we should introduce Li Yang, the person that assassinated Cyril Stanford. So the plan is to keep both of them out of the picture in protective custody. Guang has said he will make sure Chen is not a problem.'

Chaz stepped in. 'Have you located the other one that was with him? From what we could see while we were with them in the cellar, he seemed to be the mastermind behind the construction of the bomb.'

Vincent nodded as he replied, 'His name is Cui Guozhi. It was a big surprise to Guang when he discovered he was working with his son. He is a North Korean defector. If anybody was capable of making a functional suitcase nuclear device, it would have been him. This was what prompted Guang to send in his forces. Since his escape, he has been holed up in a safehouse protected by some bodyguards. He was waiting for Chen to arrange safe passage. He will not allow himself to be captured. He will fight to the death.'

Chaz nodded. 'If our plan is to work, we need him to do just that. Sergei, it's time to cut Vlad loose. Can you convince him that his best course of action would be to disappear and forget everything?'

'I will convince him that to speak of this would be very unhealthy,' Sergei said, leaving no doubt that Vlad would comply.

'Now comes the hard part. David, time for you to put your part of the plan into action. Are you sure you and Alan are okay with this? I don't have to tell you the risk you are taking. Are you sure you would not like us to lend a hand?' Chaz asked.

David looked at Alan, who nodded. 'Sometimes you have to bend the rules to get justice. This is something we are trained for. We are the tip of the spear, and it's time to show these pricks that they have messed with the wrong people.'

# 91

Sergei parked the Range Rover that he had 'requestioned' from the bomb site some distance from where Vlad was holed up. He checked the surroundings for any sign of activity, then approached the dilapidated structure when he was sure the coast was clear. He saw that Vlad's car was where he had concealed it, so he carefully made his way up the stairs to the loft's entrance. What he saw stopped him in his tracks. The door was ajar.

He approached with caution. As he pushed the door open cautiously, the smell that greeted him was familiar and did not bode well for Vlad. As he entered, he called out to see if Vlad would respond. He could see him seated in the corner when he stepped into the main area and figured he was not going to respond to anybody ever again.

Somebody had slit his throat and pulled his tongue out through the gaping wound giving him the appearance of wearing a gruesome tie. After checking that they were alone, he studied the body. He could see that whoever had done this had made him suffer for a long time before dispatching him. His hands and feet were lumps of raw flesh. The lump hammer that had been used lay on the floor beside him, covered in blood.

Sergei had no doubt who had done this. It was a typical punishment administered by the Russian mafia for anybody from their ranks that crossed them. Since Boris's death was still to be discovered, he guessed instructions had been left that if he did not return, the person to question was Vlad. It must have been one of the old crew that remembered this hideout, sadly for Vlad.

There was nothing more for him to do but wipe down anywhere he had touched and head back to let the boys know that Vlad would not be a candidate for their plan.

## 92

'We can forget about Vlad,' Sergei said, and described the condition he had found him.

Chaz shrugged. 'Well, it looks like Chi Guozhi has won the toss to be the candidate to take the fall for the assassination of Cyril. How are you going with your plans?' he asked David.

'Good, so far. We have checked out the place. Entrance is not going to be easy. The place is like a fortress, with only one entrance, and we have been told it is reinforced. If we have to force entry, it could turn ugly. These guys have no intention of being taken alive. They have no escape route.'

Chaz turned to Vincent. 'What is happening with Chen?'

'He is waiting at the embassy for the flight home. He has asked his father to return to China,' he replied.

'I presume his father has plans for him.'

Vincent nodded. 'He'll most likely arrange for him to be sent to a re-education centre. It's all about the family saving face.'

Chaz realised how hard it must be for a father to exile his son. 'Is there a way we can influence Chen to call Cui before he leaves?'

'I can ask Guang. But how can that help?'

'Well, from what David has said, smashing down the door is not a good option. So I propose that we get him to let us in,' as he began to explain his plan.

'No way. We can't let you risk your life, especially as that is exactly what he will want to do,' David interjected.

Chaz stood. 'Look. These guys tried to kill my cousin and blow my brother and me to bits. There is no way you are keeping me out of taking these guys down. In any case, do you have a better idea? If my idea works, nobody needs to get hurt other than these guys.'

Without waiting for a reply, he outlined what he wanted Guang to get his son to do.

# 93

Chen Wah Yim hung up the phone and relaxed in his comfortable chair in his office at the Chinese Embassy. Earlier that day, he had been informed that he was to fly back to Beijing today. He had just received a call to tell him a limousine was on the way to take him to his flight. Since the failure of their attack, he had been waiting for public reaction, but all focus had been on the assassination of the Deputy Prime Minister. He had tried to contact Sun Yee to find out what had gone wrong, but she had gone silent. So when news that he was returning to Chine came, he was relieved.

'Your car has arrived. Your luggage is being loaded and is waiting when you are ready, sir,' his aide informed him.

He nodded and followed him to the covered garage, where a limousine was waiting. He stepped inside and, to his utter shock, saw his father seated.

'Father, I was not expecting to see you here,' he blurted as he tried to bow.

'Please sit. This meeting is difficult enough. I am going to explain to you what is about to happen. You only have to comply, or I will have no choice but to hand the matter to Li Yang to resolve.'

Guang instructed his son. His expression was enough to cause him to gasp. 'Who?' Chen cried, trying to gather his thoughts.

'Li Yang, you know her as Sun Yee On, the woman you helped your dead friend contract to kill the Prime Minister of this country,' he replied.

'But…'

'Stop. Please don't insult me by trying to deny your involvement in all of this. I know all the sorry details. I have been watching you and your demented friends, hoping you would come to your senses. But when I discovered that madman, Chi Guozi, was involved, I had no choice but to act. Your life will be spared if you complete one last task for me. Do this, and you will board a plane that will take you to a re-education facility in central China, where you will remain until you are deemed fit to re-join our society. Refuse, well, you know the answer to that.'

His son broke down crying, 'Please forgive me, Father.'

Guang raised his hand. 'Compose yourself. I want you to call Guozhi and instruct him as follows,' and he explained what he wanted him to say.

When he finished, Chen looked at him in disbelief. 'Is this true, The Umbrella Men survived, and you want to hand one over to Guozhi?' he asked.

'Yes, that is exactly what I want you to do. Remember to tell him you are working on his rescue. And to do exactly as you ask. Just keep this guy under wraps until we see if his superiors want to interrogate him. And to wait for you to contact him.'

Hanging his head in shame, Chen took the phone to call Guozhi. As soon as he answered, he began to speak. 'It is me. I have news that those guys we left with the device survived. We have captured one of them. He will be delivered to you. You are to keep him and my man there until I contact you. He is to be unharmed. I am working on getting you out. My man will use the code word 'Tsunami'. You are to keep them on ice.'

'How long before we can move? We are running short on supplics?' he asked.

'Very soon. Just do as I ask.'

Very well,' he replied, cutting the connection.

Chen faced his father. 'I have done as you asked. What now?' he asked with his head bowed.

'I say goodbye. I don't imagine we will meet again,' he said, his voice wavering as he stepped out of the car to be replaced by two severe-looking guys.

# 94

Seated in a disguised police van not far from where Chi Guozhi was holed up, Chaz went over last-minute details with David and his so-called captor, Bill. Guang had provided Vincent and David the schematics of the apartment they were about to try and enter. If they got inside, the plan was for Bill to push the release so that David and his small team of Special Forces could storm the place and hopefully end things without anybody getting hurt. Bill had a small device disguised as a lighter that, when pressed, would alert David that the door was open.

'All safe houses we use have quick release mechanisms on the exits so they can be opened instantly if called for. There will be one release closer to the door and a hidden one behind the bar,' David informed Chaz and Bill.

'How will we recognise the release behind the bar?' Bill asked.

'It will be easy to locate. There will be a hand grip with a sign "Don't Pull". Remember, if it is ever needed in a hurry, nobody will want to waste time searching for it,' David said. Then to Chaz, 'Are you sure we can't talk you out of this?' he asked, knowing the answer.

It was Bill that replied. 'Don't worry. I will take care of him. He is one of the chaps.'

'Some family!' David groaned as he popped the back door for them to get out. 'Remember, it will be right behind you. If things get out of hand, press the device and we will blow the door. Good luck,' he said as he closed the doors, watching them head on their perilous plan.

Bill pressed the intercom on the door number he had been given. They knew from the schematics that it comprised most of the floor. He was answered with a gruff voice. 'Yes?'

He replied in his London accent, 'Tsunami.'

A second later, they heard the door click, so Bill took out his Glock that David had reluctantly provided. Prodding Chaz, he whispered, 'Let the show begin,' as they stepped through the open door.

The first thing to get their attention was the terrible state the place was in, obvious that they had not left since their arrival.

'Bring him in. I want to see if this one of those guys,' Guozhi's voice came from where he was sitting in the shadows

Bill pushed Chaz forward, making him stumble. Guozhi stood and scrutinised him. 'It is you. I found it hard to believe you could have survived. Although the nuclear device failed, the primary explosion would have destroyed everything in the chamber.'

Chaz glared at him in defiance. 'Sorry to disappoint you. But as I told your pal, Chen, my brother figured out how to defuse your little toy, and you forgot to secure the door properly in your hurry to escape with your tail between your legs.'

Guozhi's usually inscrutable face flared in anger, which was Chaz's intention. He was to create a distraction so Bill could activate the door release. But as he turned to the device to the left of the door, one of the other guys had taken up position directly in front of it with an Uzi firmly pointed at them. They had thought of this possibility and were taking no chances. Chaz quickly realised the release near the door was not an option, so he softened his approach.

'But then your boss was too clever for us and managed to locate me. Luckily, my brother had got himself back to Ireland as soon as we got out.'

Guozhi calmed. 'How did he defuse the device?'

'I will tell you everything you want to know, but I have been stuck with this guy since Chen told him to watch me until he decided what to do with me. I have been asking him for a drink, and I am not talking about water!'

Bill picked up on what he was trying to do, and said, 'That's all he goes on about. If your boss had not demanded that I keep him safe, I would have killed him myself.'

Guozhi was not convinced but still wanted to know what had happened to his bomb. 'You can have your drink. But I want to know exactly what he did,' heading in the direction of the bar. Bill tried to head him off, hoping to get behind the bar first. But Guozhi called out to one of the other guys the stop him. 'You, Englishman, stay this side of the bar. I will serve the drinks and you,' pointing at Chaz, 'you will sit facing me.'

*So far, so good, Chaz thought.*

## 95

From behind the bar, Chaz began to explain how his brother had prevented the bomb from exploding. He could see that Guozhi was fascinated by the story. At the same time, he turned his storytelling ability into an excuse for everybody to join in. Since this was the first time these guys had contact with anybody from the outside, he figured they would be more than happy to take a drink. He knew the belief that Asians did not let their hair down was a myth. They loved to party as much as anybody. He chose a bottle of fine malt whiskey and started pouring for everybody. For his plan to work, he just needed to have faith in his and Bill's drinking ability.

At first Guozhi protested, but as Chaz pointed out, this might be his last supper. He had no idea what Chaz was talking about but took a drink anyway. 'I can't believe what you describe could prevent the nuclear reaction. In theory, it could have worked. But in the hands of an amateur, it is beyond belief. All that would have achieved would be to detonate the device prematurely,' Guozhi replied as he downed another drink.

Chaz quickly refilled his glass. 'Well, from what you say, if what my brother did could not have prevented the detonation of the nuclear part, and it did not make it explode prematurely, as evidenced by my standing here talking to you, then what happened?'

Guozhi paused with his glass in front of his lips. He remained like that for what seemed to be a year. Then he downed the drink, placing it in front of the bottle for Chaz to do the honours. He replied, 'Your brother must be a genius. Because I am confident my device would have functioned perfectly if not for his intervention. So congratulations,

Irishman, you saved this country from much destruction,' and raised his glass.

Chaz joined him. 'This is for my brother, Desmond, cheers.' Swallowing it in one shot. He did not know if Guozhi believed his device would have worked or was trying to save face. It did not matter. He was starting to show the effect of the booze. 'Another bottle!' Chaz cried as they finished the third bottle.

As Guozhi placed his glass on the counter, Chaz decided it was time to act. 'Have you ever tried Irish Coffee?' he asked.

Guozhi shrugged, and Bill quickly realised what Chaz was trying to do. He quickly said, 'I was the head barman in the Savoy Hotel in Mayfair. I will make you the best one you will ever taste,' he offered.

'Let him. What harm will it do? If I try anything while he is busy, there is enough of your men to kill me ten times over.'

Guozhi nodded. 'Leave your gun over on the table and come and show us your skills.'

Chaz figured Guozhi was probably enjoying himself more than he ever had in the past. Bill swapped places with him and stepped behind the bar, at once spotting the door release. The problem was that it was placed under the counter. He would have to make an apparent move to activate it. Guozhi, unfortunately, was highly interested in watching him create his masterpiece and was watching his every move.

Bill decided to make the coffee to bide his time and hope for an opportunity to arise. The coffee machine was behind him, so he got suitable glasses out first. Realising the chances of having fresh cream were remote, he decided to improvise, putting vodka and tequila along with the whiskey and then adding sugar. He then filled the glasses with coffee and stirred them. If the real barman from the Savoy could see what he was creating, he mused, he would have shot him on the spot.

Positioning himself as close to the release as he could, he gave Chaz a slight nod to let him prepare for all hell to break loose. 'Bottoms up,' he cried as he downed the potent drink.

Bill was expecting the shock, and it still took his breath away. Guozhi and the others were not prepared for the strong drink and started to gag from the effect. He pressed the lighter while at the same time grabbing the release. Chaz ducked down at the sound of the door releasing. The door exploded open, and two marksmen entered.

Before the startled shooter, who stood to the side of the door, could react, he received a shot to the head. Before the last four guys could react, perfectly placed shots from the special forces men dropped them before they could even lift their guns.

For Chaz, all of this seemed to happen in slow motion. He had heard gunfire before, but this was something else. The noise was deafening and seemed to go on forever to him. But in fact it was all over in seconds.

As the guns fell silent, he looked behind the bar and, to his horror, saw Guozhi pointing his weapon at Bill's head. But before he pulled the trigger, Chaz launched himself across the bar, knocking the gun to one side. He landed in a heap behind the bar to see Guozhi regain his balance and point the gun at him. All Chaz could see was the gigantic hole at the end of the barrel.

Then he heard the sound of a gunshot, thinking it was all over. Then Guozhi crumpled to the ground next to him, minus most of his head. Looking up, he was greeted by the smiling face of David. 'You are welcome,' he said.

Chaz picked himself up to see that Bill was fine.

'Took you guys long enough. It looks like you were having quite the party,' David commented, eyeing all the empty bottles and glasses. Chaz started to explain, but he stopped him. 'Plenty of time for that later. Now it's time to make some noise,' as he lifted his radio to call in the official response. Deliberately on an open channel that he knew the press and freelancers monitored, he said, 'We have entered the hideout of the assumed assassin of the Deputy Prime Minister. No casualties on our side. The suspects resisted and were neutralised. Please dispatch the terrorist squad and the forensic team. There is plain evidence here of a terrorist splinter group.'

When he got a response that the teams were on their way, he turned to Chaz and Bill. 'Okay, time for you guys to make yourself scarce. We have to make sure the evidence is placed correctly.'

As he opened the case full of the "evidence" they had created back at the mansion, Bill said with a grin, 'Let's get a drink, shall we?'

# 96

Christine Wolfe listened to the reports of the discovery of Cyril's assassins who were killed in the shootout. The raid had been conducted by members of the SAS led by Chief Inspector David George. The rest of the information was sketchy. Something about a splinter group that had a particular grudge against Cyril Stanford. She was relieved that no mention of any connection between her and Cyril had surfaced.

She had to remind herself that she would soon be joining the ranks of the Australian Government as the Police Minister. Now that David George was quickly to be a hero, she would make sure to capitalise on his success. Just then, her intercom buzzed, snapping her back.

'Prime Minister on the line for you, Commissioner,' her aide told her.

'Congratulations, Christine. What a wonderful result for you and your team. Taking down the group of crazies without any casualties. Shame we could not question one of them as to their grievance with Cyril Sanford. I can't imagine what beef they had with him, can you?'

The question took her by surprise. *Is he testing me?* she wondered. 'Who knows what goes on in the minds of these people? Perhaps the evidence will shed some light on it,' she replied.

'Agreed. Now my people will be in touch with you very soon to decide to announce your new position. With that in mind, I want all information about the raid kept under wraps so we can simultaneously make a grand disclosure of you and your team's success. So not a word is to get to the press before my office announces it.'

'Of course, Prime Minister, as you wish. I will put a blanket on the whole thing until your office gives the go-ahead.'

She sat back when he disconnected the call, twirling her Dupont pen. She glanced at her watch and decided that she would finish for the day, thinking she couldn't wait to see the back of this place.

*Government House, here I come!*

# 97

Christine switched off the alarm as she entered her apartment. Turning on the lights, she headed into the kitchen and made herself a large gin and tonic. Sipping it as she returned to the living room, she froze at the sight of Chief Inspector David George and two females she did not recognise standing in front of her.

'What is the meaning of this?' she asked, trying to make sense of what was happening.

'Please forgive the intrusion. But we have to discuss a delicate matter, and we felt it should be dealt with privately,' David said, indicating she should take a seat.

'This is most irregular. How did you get in, and who are these people?' she asked, eyeing the two women standing with David.

'Now, Christine, as you well know a locked door only keeps honest people out. And I think you will agree none of us fits that description.'

His response startled her. 'I have no idea what you are talking about. I would like you to leave. You are in serious trouble for this behaviour.'

She slowly recovered her composer, then sat and began to drink her cocktail. They gave no sign that they were going to comply, so she began to examine the two women. She was sure she had never seen the Asian one before. But something about the tall, athletic-looking one struck a chord in her memory.

'This could have serious repercussions on your career, Chief Inspector, when the Prime Minister hears of this intrusion,' she said.

'He is very aware of this meeting. He is fully briefed and has been since we informed him of your involvement in the failed terrorist attack and the plan to assassinate him,' David responded. 'Before you deny it and insult our intelligence, he asked me to inform you that he will not need your services. This was just a ploy to keep you away from the press and your colleagues in London until we could explain the destruction of Chen's house and the assassination of your former lover, Cyril. It is terrible to see you so heartbroken,' he said with sarcasm.

She sat stunned by the level of information he had. Pausing, she downed her drink, placed the glass on the table, and then went on the attack. 'I have no idea where you could have come with such wild accusations. As far as I know, there was no mention of any mysterious explosion, and it would appear you have already captured and killed the assassins. I have no idea what you hope to gain. But what proof do you have to substantiate this unbelievable story?'

'We will get to that, but first, let me introduce you to my companions. This is Aurora McCormack. That name should ring a bell. She is the daughter of a murdered member of the Police Force, James McCormack.'

At once, Christine remembered where she had seen the woman before, in the picture she had provided for Cyril so the Croats could locate her. 'This is insane. What possible interest could I have with these people?' she said.

Aurora spoke. 'Well, as you can imagine, I was very anxious to find out what happened to my father. And I can tell you that your plot might have succeeded without a strange turn of events,' she said, and began to relate how her long-lost relative had found her, their efforts led to the discovery of Chen's planned attack, and the ability to foil it.

Christine turned to David. 'I want you and these people out of here at once,' she demanded.

'I am leaving shortly, but firs, you must meet Li Yang,' who responded by giving a stiff bow. 'She is the person who shot your lover, Cyril!'

# 98

Christine could not move as she stared at the expressionless face of Li Yang, turning to David. 'Why is she not under arrest?' she croaked.

'Well, as you can imagine, if that were to come out in the press, it would only help you and your misguided friend's plans. So when I told the Prime Minister I had uncovered some information that could be detrimental to the government and assist the terrorists in their plans, he decided to allow me to resolve the situation as I saw fit. Incidentally, the people we caught for the assassination were Chen's men who kindly volunteered to take the blame for Cyril's death.'

'Then who is she working for?' she asked, pointing at Li.

Li replied. 'For you, or I should say for your lover. You see, he engaged me to assassinate the Prime Minister.'

Christine gasped. 'Shi No Tenshi?' she blurted, losing her composure.

'Correct. Before your boyfriend contacted me, I had already been engaged to kill whoever asked me to kill the Prime Minister. So as soon as he engaged me, he signed his death warrant.'

Christine's survival instincts kicked in, turning to David. 'You have no proof of any of this. No prosecutor in the country would take this case. If you were to try, I would sue the department. The scandal would do far worse than what you have described.'

'You are correct. For that reason, I will leave you with the girls to work out an arrangement to resolve the dilemma,' he said, and nodded to the girls.

As David turned and walked out, Christine began to relax. So they wanted to sweep the whole thing under the carpet? she mused, eyeing the young women that had been left to negotiate with her. She composed herself, secure in the fact that she could handle them.

'Well, shall we begin?' she asked.

Aurora glanced at her watch and then addressed Li. 'She is right, and time is marching on. We should continue.' Then she addressed Christine. 'I have just one question: why did you kill my father?'

Christine almost choked on her drink. 'What are you talking about? Are you crazy? Why would I kill your father?'

Instead of replying, she placed a laptop on the table and turned the screen to face Christine. 'A picture tells a thousand words,' she said, and pressed the play button.

Christine watched in horror as a granny video appeared of her getting into James McCormack's car, wincing when it came to the part of her plunging her fountain pen into his neck and watching him die.

'How did you get this?' She could barely get the words out.

It was Li that replied. 'Your boyfriend had engaged me to do what you decided to do yourself. As always, I carry a pocket recording device. It is handy when clients want proof.'

Christine felt a little lightheaded and dizzy. She turned to Aurora, and said, 'It was an accident, I…'

Aurora cut her off. 'Please don't waste our time. Plus, you don't have much to waste.'

Her tone changed. She mocked, 'That will never stand up in court.'

Aurora nodded in agreement. 'You are probably right, but we are never going to find out. I only wanted to show you so I could see the expression on your face.'

'So what now? Are you going to arrest me, charge me with the murder of your father? And hope to get a promotion?'

Aurora shook her head. 'Can't do that. I resigned three days ago. I decided when I saw what my cousins were able to achieve what the Police Force could not. And I met somebody that feels the same way. So I decided to work outside the system. Much fewer restrictions.'

'So what now, do you intend to kill me?' she sneered, but to her ears her voice sounded a little slurred.

'Can't. You have already taken care of that. When you decided to commit suicide,' she replied.

Christine looked at her in confusion, and then a feeling of horror crept over her. 'The drink!' she gasped, eyeing the empty glass. 'How did you know what I would drink?'

'We didn't, so we just laced them all. It was only gin and vodka anyway,' she replied.

'I want you to know that the last fifteen minutes of the poison that my friend kindly provided will be terrorising. You will begin to feel it difficult to breathe. It is a derivative of snake venom that paralyses your respiratory system. So you are going to choke to death.'

Forty minutes later, the girls were on their way back to the mansion after watching Christine expire in the most painful way possible. Li Yang turned to Aurora as they drove. 'Do you feel like you thought you could?' she asked.

Aurora thought for a moment and then replied, 'To be truthful, I was so caught up in vengeance that I did not know what to expect. The strange thing was, when I saw her go, I just felt relief. That woman did not deserve to take up any more oxygen.'

Li Yang smiled and handed her the Dupont fountain pen she had taken from Christine's cold hand. She gave her new partner a reassuring squeeze on her arm.

'We will be fine,' she said, bringing a smile to Aurora's face.

# 99

The Office of the Prime Minister had asked David and Alan to attend a special ceremony in Parliament House in two days' time.

The event was treated like a special event. Not just for the broadcast but their interest in how the Prime Minister would spin the events that Vincent and the group had concocted. Successful as they were. It still depended on how the public perceived it.

They were all relaxing at the Suarez's mansion with their extended family. Li and Aurora watched the events unfold, each discovering feelings they had never experienced, each processing them in their own way.

The presenter began the event by announcing the Prime Minister on the dais. He walked out to tumultuous applause from the assembled crowd. Nobody seemed to notice the increased security as they enjoyed the warm summer day.

He raised his hand for silence and then began to speak. 'My fellow Australians and our many visitors from around the globe, it was a pleasure to talk to you today. I will start by telling you why I needed to hold this announcement. There have been many theories, speculations, and crazy conspiracies about why our colleague was killed in such a brutal matter. So for that reason, I have called this conference. I will begin by announcing the man responsible for bringing this ugly event to a swift conclusion. Inspector David George. Please join me.'

David strode quickly to the Prime Minister. He was feeling very awkward but kept himself composed. They shook hands to thunders applause. They waited, still shaking hands until it began to subside.

Mick Parker began to speak. 'As you may have heard, the passing of our Police Commissioner Christina Wolfe suddenly. My understanding is that she had no immediate family. But her colleagues here will miss her dedication, and she will be sorely missed. But we are here for you to hear from the person himself, Head of the Major Crime Squad, David George.'

David composed himself and then began to speak. 'I have been instructed to tell you as much as possible how we apprehend the people who perpetrated the crime against Cyril Stanford during an ongoing investigation I was carrying out when it was brought to my attention that there was to be an attempt on the life of an essential member of the Government. The source of this information cannot be disclosed. Still, as far as we were concerned, we felt it was credible. Only after our minister's assassination were we able to establish exactly where these people were. You already know that we located their hideout, which we surrounded and gave they the opportunity to surrender. But it became obvious they had no intention of been take alive.' He took a breath, then continued. 'What I can disclose was their motive, disturbed as it was. From documents, we discovered their hideout and the information we had received. They had a deep hatred for the influence of, and I quote, "The ruling class", which they believed originated in Great Britain and Cyril Stanford had been chosen as a perfect example of what they despised. A successful businessman from England came here and tried to impose his values. He was unlucky.'

He paused as Vincent had instructed for the words to sink in. There was silence for a moment then the crowd slowly began to show how they felt about The Right Honourable Cyril Stanford. The cheers started slowly but quickly became deafening.

David raised his hand in acknowledgement, smiling as Vincent's prediction evolved as he said it would. The 'Tall Poppy Syndrome' was alive and well from what he could gather. The public's dislike for Cyril Stanford in life was apparent even in death.

Michael Parker re-joined David on the stage, bringing even more reaction from the crowd. He raised his hand for silence. ' There is only one more task I have to perform for today, and I will ask David's right-hand man to join us. Please welcome Detective Sergeant Allan Moffatt.'

Allan's massive frame appeared as he hurried to join his partner. Mick welcomed him and then indicated for the stand at his side. His aide appeared with a small case he placed in front of the Prime Minister.

'Today I wish to announce due to the untimely death of the Police Commissioner Christina Wolfe.' He paused for a minute silence. Then continued, 'Therefore, as a result of this vacancy and their excellent work in bringing this terrible event to a close, I have the great pleasure of appointing David George, our new Police Commissioner and Allan Moffatt as his deputy.'

He indicated for them to step forward to receive their new badge. With them hanging around their necks, they turned to receive another resounding cheer.

It was playing out like a Sergio Leon movie, and the media was lapping it up. The press had reported from all over. Even the top networks in the USA had sent teams to cover it.

Chaz said to Vince, 'That went exactly as you predicted.'

'That's what they pay me the big bucks,' Vince replied with a smug look on his face. Looking around the room, he asked, 'Where is Des?'

'Yes, he has been acting strange for the last few days when we decided on our plan for me, and Bill to go on the raid. I was surprised he did not put up his hand. You know him always wanting to be charging in first,' Chaz replied. 'As soon as the raid was over, he told me he would be gone for a few days. When I asked him where he was going, he said there was something he wanted to check out. I was so preoccupied that I forgot to ask Maria if she know what he was doing.' He saw her over Vince's shoulder. She was talking to Diego. 'Let's go ask her now.'

As they wandered over to her, she appeared very guarded. 'He would not tell me. He just said there was something he wanted to check out. When I asked if there was any danger, he assured me not and convinced me it would be better if he went alone and that he would only be a few days. I spoke to him on the phone yesterday, and he assured me he would be home soon.'

They spent the rest of the evening discussing the upcoming visit to the Prime Minister's private residence at Kirribilli House. Suddenly, Maria rushed into the room, her phone clutched in her hand. 'Des is coming home tomorrow and has requested everybody to be here. He had some important news!' When they tried to get more information, she shrugged. 'You know as much as I do. All I could get out of him was that he suggested everybody held on to their hats. What does he mean by that?'

# 100

The entire extended family were assembled in the living room of the Suarez mansion awaiting Des's return. Everybody was speculating about what his mysterious news was. For the first time, his brothers had no idea. Usually, his schemes and misadventures were pretty obvious. But this time, he had them baffled. The fact that he had kept Maria in the dark added more mystery because since they had gotten together, they had been inseparable.

Diego had sent a driver to fetch him from the airport. He had asked that only Maria come to greet him. Now the sound of the car arriving snapped them to attention.

Two minutes later, Des came into the room. He had a big smile on his sunburned face, yet only his brothers noticed he was holding back, something he did only when he was worried that he had screwed up. Everybody crowded around to welcome him back and bombard him with questions. Finally, he put his hand up to speak.

'Can you give me a minute to get a breath and perhaps a drink? I am parched.'

Chaz handed him a beer, then said, 'Okay, enough of the drama. You have got your audience now out with what's going on.'

Nodding in agreement, he took a seat, finishing his beer in one swallow. Then spoke. 'It all started with the shoe...'

# 101

**COOBER PEDY**
**THREE DAYS AGO**

Des wiped the sleep out of his eyes as he dismounted the bus. He had deliberately taken this form of transport as he wanted to arrive unannounced. He had made a reservation at the Desert Cave Hotel, which they had stayed at what seemed a lifetime ago. The girl at reception recognised him at once.

'Where is the wife?' she inquired.

'She is not my wife,' he muttered. 'Is the car I rented here yet?'

Not to be deterred, she nodded, handing him the key to his room and the keys for the rental. 'If you don't put a ring on that pretty girl's hand, she will be snatched up,' she added.

'Thanks for the advice. I will get right on as soon as I get back,' he replied sarcastically.

He dropped the small bag with his belongings in his room and headed outside to where the rental car was parked. It was a four-wheel drive Jeep, as requested. Then he headed for a mining supply store to pick up a few things he thought he might need. Satisfied, he set out on his task.

He was heading back to the abandoned claim where Steve had brought them. Something had been nagging at him, and he decided that the only way he would be satisfied would be to check it out. He had not said anything to Chaz in case he was on a wild goose chase. Also, with all that was going on back at the mansion, he was happy to handle it all by himself.

He located the place he was looking for after a few wrong turns. Everything looked the same to him, deserted claims with abandoned bits of broken equipment. He could almost sense the disappointment and despair that the miners must have felt. Digging for weeks on end, hoping to make their fortune, only to have their hopes repeatedly dashed.

He parked the Jeep close to the edge of where the outline of the original mining had taken place. The area had not been touched since he was last here. He went to the edge of the pit where he had nearly fallen the last time, looking down into the darkness. Since he had found the woman's shoe, he wanted to check that Rosa Herrero was not lying at the bottom.

He fixed a strong rope he had bought to the winch fitted to the front of the Jeep. He strung it over the lip of the pit and dropped it down. When he heard it hit the bottom, he activated the winch with the hand control, retracting the rope until the end reappeared. Then, making a loop to place his foot, he stepped over the edge, balanced himself, and activated the winch to descend into the darkness.

He touched down after only a few seconds. The pit was only about three to four metres deep. Stepping off, he stood for a moment, then switched on the powerful lamp he had purchased along with the rope and shone it around, fearing what he might find. But there was nothing except for some old pieces of digging equipment. He could not see any sign of a body. After searching for clues, he finally decided nothing was to be found.

He stepped back onto the loop on the rope, started the winch, and began his assent, shining the lamp at the wall as he went up. He was passing what remained of the ladder when something caught his eye. Stopping the winch, he reached over to retrieve what he had seen. It was a piece of cloth. As he examined it, her could see it was part of a woman's dress.

He stepped out of the pit and removed the rope from the winch, then sat and began to rewind the events of the last time they had visited here with Steve Yakov. The last thing he remembered happening was nearly falling into the pit, and as a result, he discovered the shoe. But instead of showing interest, all that had concerned Steve was getting them back for their flight.

'Time for some answers,' he said to himself as he jumped into the Jeep and headed back to town.

# 102

Steve answered the door as soon as he knocked. 'Desmond, you are back.' He was stating the obvious with a big smile, but the expression on Des's face told him something was wrong. He stared at him for a moment, then said, 'I guess this is not a social visit,' inviting him in. 'I assume that you found the people you were looking for,' he said as he offered Des a beer.

'Yes. They had an interesting story. I am not sure how much you know. They were surprised that you never tried to contact them.'

Steve looked at the ground. 'I followed their success in the press and online. I did not think they would want a reminder of their time in this hell hole.'

'But that was not your reason for not contacting them, was it?' Des asked.

'I guess you did not come to tell me you located your relations. It was the shoe, wasn't it?' he asked.

Des nodded. 'The shoe and your lack of interest in it. I had to check if Rosa was at the bottom of that hole in the ground.'

'You thought I had something to do with her disappearance?'

'No, but considering what had happened that night there was a possibility that she was the victim also,' Des replied, then continued. 'So I decided to have a look.'

'You went to the claim to check it out?' he asked.

'Yes, and went down to look, but she wasn't there. But you already know that.'

He pulled out the piece of cloth he had found and handed it to Steve. He took it in his hand. 'Where did you find this?' he asked, rubbing the piece of material between his fingers.

'On what was left of the ladder. She must have snagged it when she climbed out, that was when she lost the shoe, correct?' he asked.

He slumped his head. 'No, she lost it when that bastard Felipe hit her over the head and tossed her into the pit. Luckily, he hit her with the flat of the shovel. She was knocked unconscious, which probably saved her in the fall. Anyway, she came to later and climbed out. That's where I found her and took her back to my place,' he replied.

He stood and fetched a bottle of whiskey and two glasses. As they drank, he told Des how he had searched for Felipe, knowing there was only one direction he could go as the main road would have taken through the main street, somewhere he would have wanted to avoid. Then went on to explain how he had followed a trail that headed north. He discovered Felipe's body lying beside his truck with a bullet hole in his head about a few hundred kilometres up the track.

'One of the Nightshift probably killed him for what he had in his pockets. Saved me the job,' he said, downing another shot of whiskey.

Des decided to explain how they had discovered what happened to Felipe without going into too much detail. 'You were right. One of the Nightshift had robbed him and used the information and documents to blackmail Diego and Monica Suarez. So what became of Rosa Herrero?' Des asked.

Steve was silent for a moment. Then raised his head and spoke. 'Rosa Herrero is dead I am sad to say,' he replied.

'What happened to her?' Des asked.

'I think perhaps my wife should be here for this. You have never met her. She was away visiting friends when you were with your wife.'

'She is not my wife!' he said, unable to contain himself.

Steve ignored him and called for his wife. 'Rita, can you come in here? There is someone I would like you to meet,' he shouted into the back of the house.

A few moments later, an attractive woman in her early sixties appeared at the door, wiping her hand's in a dishtowel.

'I am just making dinner,' she announced, then noticed her guest.

'Sorry, I did not know we had guests,' she apologised, approaching him with an outstretched hand.

'This is Des. He was one of the people I told you about who came here searching for their relatives, Diego and Monica Suarez. This is my wife, Rita.' He indicated for her to take a seat beside him and continued to explain. 'They found them in Melbourne, and Des has told me the whole family has been united. Now Des has returned to find out what happened to Rosa Herrero. I felt you should be here as he hears what happened.'

# 103

## THE SUAREZ MANSION
## MELBOURNE

Desmond paused in his story, causing an eruption. 'You can't stop now. What happened to her?' Chaz demanded, with a chorus of agreement from everyone else.

He took a much need drink and then raised his hand for quiet. 'All right. But I felt that instead of hearing it from me. I invited Steve Yakov and his wife Rita so you can hear the story firsthand.'

'You brought them here? Where are they?' Vince asked.

'If you pair would shut up for a minute, I will tell you. They are waiting outside with Maria. I clued her in before we arrived. I will tell her to bring them in.'

He went to the door. 'Maria, you can come in now. We are ready.' He stepped aside as Maria escorted the couple into the expectant stares of the assembled crew. Then he did the introductions. 'Everybody, this is Steve Yakov and his wife Rita, please make them welcome, and we will get to the story shortly.'

He introduced them individually. Proceeding around the room, they arrive at Diego and Monica. He introduced Monica first. She shook Rita's hand, and as their eyes made contact, they paused with their eyes locked for what seemed to be an eternity. Then Monica gave out a croak and fainted on the spot.

As they placed her on a couch, Chaz grabbed his brother. 'What the hell is happening here?' Then the penny dropped. 'It's her, isn't it?'

Des nodded. 'But why don't we let them explain,' indicating the concerned couple. 'Let's hear their story. From them.'

By this time, Monica had recovered from her faint. Her husband comforted her as Steve began their story. 'As you have heard so far. After discovering Felipe's body, I kept Rosa's whereabouts a secret. Not that was much of a problem in a place like Coober Pedy. Most people had something to hide, and everybody kept to themselves. So I decided to nurse her back to health, and when she could travel, I decided to relocate to Port Augusta for a while until the dust settled. Please remember that I did not know that Diego and Monica would turn the Herrero name into a household name in Australia at that time. That's when I came up with a plan.' He paused to look at his wife, who nodded for him to continue. 'My life in that hell hole before Rosa came into my life was pretty boring, and I watched many movies. Back then, you rented them, and I loved the old ones. That's where I got the idea for my plan.' Steve paused, then continued. 'It was one of my favourites, an old classic, *The Day of the Jackal*, starring Edward Fox.'

He glanced at Rosa again to see her shaking her head. 'Sorry, Rosa always tells me to get to the point when I tell stories. It is probably because this one involves you guys,' pointing at Monica and Diego. Clearing his throat, he continued. 'In the film, he creates a false identity by visiting a church graveyard and locating someone born about the same time as him but who had died very young. He then went to the church posing as a relation and got a copy of the birth certificate. So that is what I did. I returned to Coober Pedy and, in the local graveyard, located the grave of a baby girl that had died at birth. The date suited. Luckily, the local priest was someone I had done some favours for in the past, so he provided me with a copy of the birth certificate. I had a hard time convincing Rosa that it was our only option. With the murder of that thug, George Pratt, hanging over your heads. We knew that Rosa Herrero could not reappear without questions being asked. Finally, she agreed.'

Des jumped in. 'You never explained how you managed to create the new identity?'

He smiled. 'You have to remember that back then, there were no computers, and many of the arrivals did not understand the laws here, with many having scant information about their life before coming here. Our story to the authorities was Rosa, or as she was calling herself by this time, Rita Scarpa, as that was the name on the gravestone, was that her parents had immigrated here from Italy, and she was born here. We told them they had lived in Coober Pedy and had died very young to leave Rita under the care of the church. And the only document she had was her birth certificate. They accepted the story, and we got a driving licence and even a passport. So as you can see from that point on, Rosa Herrero was dead, and Rita Scarpa was resurrected.'

For the first time, Rita spoke. 'What he did not tell you is that he saved my life. And we soon fell in love. When he asked me to marry him, Rita Yakov became a whole person again,' she said, hugging her husband.

Monica could not contain herself and jumped up to join in the embrace. Diego followed suit. They burst into tears of joy. The rest of the evening was taken up with bringing everybody up to date with the series of events that got them to this point. Monica and Diego gave their story and how what had happened made them decide to bring their children home and explain to them face to face what had happened and how they had come by their names, allowing them to determine what they wanted them to do.

Rita encouraged them to do what pleased them as far as she was concerned. Felipe and Rosa Herrero from the past was just a bad dream that needed to be left in the past. She insisted on being called Rita. Rosa Herrero was dead as far as she was concerned.

This prompted another round of hugs and the Savage brothers stepped outside to give them all time to process the staggering news. 'You never cease to amaze me. How did you figure out she was still alive?' Vince asked Des, pouring him a fresh drink.

'I could not get out of my mind the strange behaviour from Steve when I found the lady's shoe. I figured that when he didn't react, he must have known what had happened to Rosa. At first, I thought he knew she was dead and did not want the whole affair to be raked up again. But then, after he directed us to Monica and Diego, I could not see him helping us if he was covering up her death. So I decided to check it out, and you know the rest.'

Vince and Chaz just looked at each other and then raised their glasses at him. 'To the saviour of countries and lost souls.'

# 104

**SYDNEY**
**ONE WEEK LATER**

They had all been invited to an unofficial dinner with the Prime Minister at Kirribilli house. The Herreros were also invited, which raised the subject of how they would deal with the name change. To their surprise, the children took the news quite casually.

Their son spoke first. 'Mum, our history has always been a bit of a mystery. Remember, so whatever you choose is good for me.'

Christina burst in. 'And me, It has taken me enough time to get the South Africans to pronounce the name I have now. I don't need the grief!' she exclaimed with a smile. 'I want to meet these crazy Irishmen that made all this happen. I could use someone like that back in South Africa. The police are usually too corrupt to trust.'

So it was decided they would leave sleeping dogs lie.

Upon arrival at Kirribilli House, Michael Parker greeted them like long-lost friends, welcoming them into his home. Everybody was enjoying themselves and after dinner was finished, they broke up into smaller groups. Christina Herrero had latched on to Charlie and told him the challenges they were encountering in South Africa as it battled with gang warfare and corruption. Vincent rescued him before he got talked into helping.

Aurora and Li had come as a couple. Something that was become apparent. It had been decided that she should use the name Sun Yee On as her real identity could not be revealed to the Prime Minister.

They had stepped out to a magical view of the majestic Sydney harbour and the famous bridge, with the Opera House as a backdrop. Even Vincent was impressed. 'Maybe I should look at opening up a practice here. I could handle this,' seeing himself entertaining in a similar style.

Michael Parker called for attention. 'I am in the position of having to thank so many people for helping avert something David prohibited me from speaking about for, and I quote "Security reasons", and I thought I was the boss! But it turns out that matters relating to national security are on a strictly need-to-know basis. My reason for the long introduction is that if I omit to thank anybody, it will be because I have not been told about you. With that said, I must again thank all the efforts that David 'Rambo' George and Allam Moffatt have made to prevent a trial by press and Twitter. They managed to capture or eliminate those responsible and keep it from being scandalised. But to do that, he has had tremendous help from three brothers who, without their constant search for their relatives despite putting themselves in peril, persisted not only in their search but decided to resolve their problems which included an attack on this country. Yet as you already know, David has sealed all of your involvement to protect you from repercussions. But that was not going to stop me from inviting you all here to thank you personally so long as you remember that if you speak about it, I will have you shot!'

Everyone laughed, and he continued. 'I will begin by thanking a couple of guys who have also become good friends. They are Vincent Savage and Bill Heart. I was playing catch-up when all of this came to a head. They stepped in on Allan's insistence, saying, I quote, "Leave it to these guys to figure it out and then do as they direct. I promise you will be happy with the result." They are the ones that discovered the depth this went. So, if you choose to set up shingle here in Australia, I can assure you there will be no red tape,' and he finished with a toast to all concerned.

Later, Chaz, Vincent and Bill were observing the excitement from all the families. Christine had captured Des, trying to get him interested in the problems she was encountering in South Africa. She had picked up on his use of a certain phrase, and they overheard her say something along the lines that she'd toss him for it. Maria, who also saw, was keeping a careful eye on her.

'Are they still denying that their relationship is not serious?' Vince asked.

Bill answered. 'They are both as bad as each other in that regard. Yet I would not want to be the person that tried to get between them.'

Chaz looked at Des, revelling in all the attention he was getting and standing there looking the part of some swashbuckling viking with his long flowing blond hair. He turned to Vince. 'Did you ever establish from Chen Senior the possibility of that bomb exploding, regardless of what Des did?'

'Well, he said until he discovered the bomb maker from North Korea, Cui Guozhi, was involved. His people convinced him that it could not work, but the mention of that guy changed things. Hence he sent the team to stop him. As to what Des did, he said that, technically, what he had done could have worked. The problem is that it has yet to be tried. So as Chen said, perhaps what he did prevented the device from exploding. We will never know. Do you think we should say anything to him?'

Chaz looked at his younger brother, enjoying himself, then replied, 'No way. If we do that, he will never believe anything he sees in the cinema again!' as they burst into laughter.

# ?

## EPILOGUE

**LONDON**
**ONE MONTH LATER**

Lincoln George Foster was in his office licking his wounds. All his carefully laid plans were in disarray. Here in England, support for his group had vanished, not helped by the Brexit debacle. In Australia, the news was even worse. Following the assassination of Cyril Stanford, the government and Prime Minister were enjoying the highest approval rating since the Federation was ratified in 1901. Then that stupid woman, Christine Wolfe, decided to take her own life.

'Probably for the best. Time to wipe the slate clean and start again,' he muttered.

Picking up the phone, he called for his driver to collect him and take him home. He gathered his laptop, intending to have a relaxing evening connecting with his remaining followers. He did not doubt his ability to regroup and emerge stronger.

He exited his office to see his parked car awaiting his arrival. Out of the corner of his eye, he saw an attractive young woman with her attention fixed on the phone she held in her hand. She looked like any other tourist following a map. But she wasn't looking where she was walking, and he had no time to get out of her way. They collided, with her grabbing his hand for support. He felt a sharp sting before she regained her balance.

She began apologising profusely as he rubbed his hand. 'Sorry, I think I must have scratched you,' displaying her long colourful nails.

Then she turned and walked off. He watched her stride off on her incredibly long legs, then brought himself to the present with a sigh. As he stepped into his car, he rubbed his hand again.

Aurora crossed the road as his car pulled away. She turned the next corner to find Li Yang waiting.

'How did it go?' she asked.

'Just as you said it would. He barely noticed it,' handing Li the retractable syringe she had given her earlier.

'The clock is ticking,' she said, glancing at her watch. 'Shall we finish up back at the hotel?' she asked Aurora, locating a drain to dispose of the syringe. Seeing the look of concern on Aurora's face, she said, 'Don't worry. By now any residue will be harmless. Plus, the syringe itself will self-destruct in an hour or so.'

'Just like *Mission Impossible*,' she said.

Li smiled. 'What we have just done sure was possible,' she replied, and hailed a passing cab.

The cabbie dropped them at the entrance of the Four Seasons Park Lane Hotel in Hampton Place. Inside, they went directly to their suite. All paid for by their employer for their first assignment since deciding to form an alliance.

They had changed into some comfortable clothes and Aurora had ditched the wig she was wearing. They were lounging on the enormous circular couch facing the window with champagne in hand. Sun glanced at her watch.

'It's about time,' she said.

Aurora refilled the glasses. 'Is there any chance they will discover the poison?' she asked.

'Impossible, it is a synthetic derivative of snake venom that causes the heart of its victim to shut down instantly. This version takes about one hour of injection to do its job and passed out of the system. This makes it act slower, which sadly makes the effect very uncomfortable, until death,' she replied with some sarcasm. 'How do you feel?' she asked her friend, as she clinked glasses.

Aurora thought for a moment. 'Satisfied. Not for any reason of revenge. But rather having been involved in delivering a bit of rough justice.'

'Best answer. I could not have said it better,' Li said, then was quiet for a moment. 'You know, I'm thinking of retiring "Li Yang" and her side business. How about we stick with my preferred name, Sun Yee On?'

'Sounds great. But before we do anything else, I need the longest shower ever,' Aurora declared.

'Me too. Who is going first?' Sun Yee On cried.

Aurora smiled, then cried, 'I'll toss you for it!'

www.ingramcontent.com/pod-product-compliance
Lightning Source LLC
Chambersburg PA
CBHW070837250626
47159CB00003B/819